THE EVIL STAR

Jed Crane returns to Indian Stone, but he carries the cruel scars of life in a Federal prison. Once home, he thinks, he can cast off a dark, tormented past. Instead, he finds a broken family and a ranch in the clutches of a corrupt lawman. Jed fights to regain his ranch and the last of its cattle. Then a powerful storm surges in from the Glass Mountains. In the ruins of Indian Stone, Jed has his final confrontation. Now it is kill or be killed.

CALEB RAND

THE
EVIL STAR

Complete and Unabridged

LINFORD
Leicester

First published in Great Britain in 2000 by
Robert Hale Limited
London

First Linford Edition
published 2002
by arrangement with
Robert Hale Limited
London

British Library CIP Data

Rand, Caleb
    The evil star.—Large print ed.—
Linford western library
    1. Western stories
    2. Large type books
    I. Title
    823.9'14 [F]

    ISBN 0–7089–9806–2

Published by
F. A. Thorpe (Publishing)
Anstey, Leicestershire

Set by Words & Graphics Ltd.
Anstey, Leicestershire
Printed and bound in Great Britain by
T. J. International Ltd., Padstow, Cornwall

This book is printed on acid-free paper

1

Chimney Point

It was nearly seven o'clock when Jedediah Crane crossed the rail tracks of Chimney Point. He was tall, slim built, and rode easy. He wore jinglebob spurs, and his stovepipe boots worked expertly in the stirrups. As he turned into the main street, a breeze snatched at his buckskin coat revealing a long-barrelled Walker Colt.

The buildings appeared temporary and distressed by their makeshift construction. To a stranger it was somewhere at the end of the line; a raw cow town, that offered little in the way of comfort or accommodation. But that was all right by Jed Crane, he was passing through, and not looking for either.

Ahead of him was the mail rider's

depot, and a sheriff's office. To the side, was a blacksmith's shop and livery stables. Set back, way beyond the cow pens, was an area that Jed sensed, rather than had knowledge of. He cast an eye over the tents and ramshacks that provided entertainment; a lair for whoring, gambling and gunplay. Chimney Point was where law and order came second to pleasure, for trail-weary buckaroos.

He crabbed the horse across the mud ruts, and up to the steps of a saloon. It had rusting metal characters that spelled out SILVER RIBBON nailed to one side of the door. He looked at the Appaloosa and nodded at the hitch; it was only a gesture of restraint. He held up the palm of his hand and told it to be quiet. 'Wait here, I may be needing you.'

Inside, aromas of tobacco and oaked-whiskey mingled with the 'cling' of Texas Longhorn. There were five or six tables, and each one had a fat, tallow candle sitting in the centre, but like the world outside, everything appeared to be dust-caked and colourless.

Jed walked slowly to the bar, and asked the bartender for a beer. He guessed it might be a mistake, changed his mind, and settled for whiskey. He lifted a hard-boiled egg ftom a wooden bowl, bit off the top, and dipped the bright yolk into the fearsome spirit. For anyone interested enough, this was how he took his food. He stared at the mirror behind the counter for a minute or so, until his dark eyes made contact with the reflections of two men sitting behind him.

One of them was a young, half-breed Comanche, swarthy, with dull black eyes. A livid scar bent from the side of his left eye to the cleft of his top lip. But the other had a pale face and long white hair; his eyes had the emptiness of someone who could hurt for pleasure.

There was a bottle of whiskey on the table and two glasses. For a long time, the older man looked at the reflection of Jed before he spoke. He dabbed his mouth and nose against the sleeve of his thin coat, oblivious to the scab of shine that stretched from wrist to elbow.

'Hey, boy. I reckon I know you from somewhere,' he called. 'Turn around and have a good look. You might remember me.'

Jed turned and looked at both men with obvious indifference.

The man's voice was charged with hostility. 'A few years back, an' a ways west o' here. You've put on a few pounds, but nothin' else seems to have gotten any better.'

Jed remained silent, his cool stare lingered, but his stance hardened.

The half-breed grinned malevolently. 'Looks like yer friend don't remember ya, Lepe.'

Lepe Scranton showed his quid-stained teeth. 'Sure he does. I'll just help him on a bit.' He unwound himself from the table and stepped forward.

When the man approached him, Jed realized he was pushing for a fight.

'Yep, I seen ya before. Galesburg in '63. You an' them other John Rebs. It was seein' ya in the mirror. I recognized yer narrow back . . . not even wide enough fer the yellow stripe.'

At the mention of Galesburg, a haunting shudder ran through Jed. He spoke with a thin, sardonic smile across his face. 'And I recognize your mouth. It reminds me of the hell-hole in the ground I spent most o' my time crouched over.'

Scranton moved in close, but the 'breed was suddenly behind him, holding him back, his scar tight and livid. 'You're right about Lepe's mouth, friend. Gets him into no end o' trouble.'

As the memory of the miserable, diseased stockade returned to Jed, Scranton shook away the 'breed's restraining arm. 'That's a big pistol you're wearin', cottonseed; rare in these parts. Not gonna object to me takin' a closer look, are yer?'

'Why don't you see what happens

when you try,' Jed suggested quietly, but Scranton took no heed.

As he reached for the Colt, Jed drove the point of his elbow up and into the man's mouth. Scranton didn't make a sound, other than a short, mushy grunt. In the same instant, Jed lashed out with his foot at the 'breed who was leaving the gun-taking to Scranton. He was surprised by Jed's retaliation, and only had time to stare. Jed's foot caught him low in the belly and, as he folded, Jed snapped his left arm around his neck. He wrenched hard, using the man's body as a buffer. He staggered two steps backward, trying to see what Scranton, or the barman, or anyone else was going to do. With a crushing throat and a busted gut, the 'breed was turning into a dead weight. Jed loosed him, and with his right hand swung up his Colt.

As the man crumpled at his feet, Jed fired a shot across the bar. The bullet smashed its way through the bowl of eggs, whiskey bottle and a cluster of empty glasses. The barman had retreated, scared for his life in the uproar. The few remaining customers sat open-mouthed and fearful at their tables.

Scranton lunged awkwardly at Jed, but slipped in the spilled booze and smashed glass. He cursed, and pitched head first into a chair and across a small table. The 'breed choked, and from the floor, raised his gun. But any reaction was spent and, as his finger curled to the trigger, his wrist was slammed by the barrel of Jed's Walker Colt.

Jed made for the open door, kneeing the side of Scranton's head in his dash to the street. The Appaloosa was standing nervous, but ready, and Jed threw himself into the saddle. He drove his heels deep into the horse's flanks, and at the end of the main street, he swung south. He thought about his imminent return to Texas, and set the Appaloosa into an unrestrained gallop. It was time to get to the border.

★ ★ ★

He knew he was being trailed, ever since he'd crossed the Pecos River. They'd stayed far off, keeping their distance, but Jed was tired of their grinding presence, tired of looking to his back and cold-harbour nights. He hoped to make the Rio Conchos tomorrow, or maybe the next day. If his pursuers really meant business, they'd make a try for him then, or thereabouts. On the outskirts of the *llano*, law enforcement was the guts to pull a trigger, but in Texas there was imposed federal law and the Rangers. The Texas Rangers were devoted to the suppression of banditry — a special force, unrelenting and tough. Not many lawbreakers went up against them.

Jed couldn't think of any reason why he should be hunted. There'd been a minor skirmish in Tularosa, even a reward out for him for a while, but that was a few years back. The man who'd tried to collect, ended his life face down in the San Andreas lava beds. The one who'd sponsored him, got a bullet in the throat after cheating at a game of faro.

At the base of a shallow depression, Jed dismounted. He left his horse nosing dirt while he crawled up the slope of the bluff. He hunkered down, dipping his Stetson against the brilliance of the big sky. To the east, the plateau shimmered, yellow and dusty. There was nothing that moved under the searing heat, and he turned his attention west.

A mile in the distance, an arroyo curled between low ridges, its course marked by gnarled shrub and bunch-grass. As he watched, small peppery clouds burst from a stand of birch. It was what Jed needed to know, and he scrambled more positively back down the bluff. Whoever it was still following him had just scared a few junco finches from their squat.

He was safe enough for a while, and he let the Appaloosa off at a canter.

They wouldn't approach him before dark; plenty of time for Jed to ponder their identities. They could be amity travellers, keeping out of sight because it was a good idea to. West of the Brazos, a lot of folk moved around that way. They either weren't looking for trouble, or they'd already found it.

But somehow he didn't think that. During the last two days he'd changed course half-a-dozen times, but still they trailed him. A sense of foreboding nicked away inside him, and again he considered his return to Texas. He wondered whether anyone knew about him, what he'd done, where he'd been. No patriotic, or 'tribal' Texan would suffer him. The brawl he'd endured in Chimney Point was a reminder, and Jed wondered how long before the next ugly conflict.

★　★　★

For nearly ten miles they galloped, until they met the breezes drifting across the plain, then they slowed to a walk until the very last of the day's light had slipped away. Jed dismounted and let the reins drop from his fingers. He walked into the cool, blue night, and felt the warmth of the Appaloosa's nose rubbing the small of his back. It was a tag of loyalty he needed.

There was supper for him and his horse, and there was water from the Pecos arroyos. He caked up chopped apple and clover honey for the horse, and for himself, bacon and yellow peas and coffee over a bravado fire. He wanted something hot, and before he did something about being a quarry.

When he'd eaten, he set about fixing his bedroll. He pressed a saddle pouch and dry mesquite under the blanket, and set his Stetson against the skirt of his saddle. Against the dying embers of his camp-fire, and under the thin moonlight, the deception looked believable from a dozen paces or more.

Jed looked cautiously around him. It was full dark, and a lone coyote barked from far across the plain. After checking his ammunition, he led the Appaloosa off a short distance. He made a loose hobble, then moved back to the far side of the ebbing fire. He kicked out a hide in the brush and, resting the Colt in the crook of his arm, he curled up and waited.

Three of them came not long after midnight, two together, and one keeping his distance. They'd ridden to within thirty feet of the smoking embers when the Appaloosa sniffed them out. It curled its lips and let out one screaming whinny; Jed withered.

He used both hands to steady his Colt as the fusillade of gunshots poured into the ground around his small camp-fire.

Jed could see them then, the pair he'd tangled with in Chimney Point. But he had no time to think about it as they jolted their horses forward.

From where he was holed-up, Jed heard them clearly. The young half-breed called out, 'It'll be a long time afore he wakes, Buck. Must've hit him three, four times.'

There was a low response from the man who remained further back in the darkness. 'Don't take no chances, Gato. I can't risk one o' them Cranes turnin' up.'

The mention of his own name had Jed immediately confused and shaken. He squinted, his eyes aching to see more clearly.

Scranton sat a big roan, and he held a Winchester. The 'breed followed him closely, with a handgun. They pulled up just outside the glow of the fire. Scranton shook his head anxiously. 'If he lives, it'll be trouble later on.'

The 'breed fired another two rounds into the bundle that was Jed Crane.

In the crushed, still silence that followed, Jed winced at the sweet, acrid bite of powder smoke that ribboned around his face. He watched spellbound, as Scranton rammed the barrel of his rifle into the inert form; gripped his Colt even tighter, as the tall,

13

white-haired man yelled wretchedly into the night, 'It's not him. The scum-suckin' mudsill pig ain't here. It's just a bundle a rags.'

Jed stood and fired then. 'You miserable bastards,' he yelled. It was too dark for him to make a killing shot, but it was close, and Scranton dashed the roan away in alarm. Jed fired and shouted again, but the horse and rider were already lost to the night.

Jed dropped to one knee. The 'breed was holding his horse on a tight rein as it snorted and bucked. Jed could see that in remaining, the young 'breed had some inbred grit. The 'breed gripped his horse tightly with his legs, and backing slightly, fired two, quick shots deliberately at Jed.

They'd fired at the same time, but Jed had the blood edge.

The 'breed knew he'd made a mistake and, as he rocked, with a bullet tearing his chest apart, he grinned, shallow and vainly. He pushed his gun back into his holster, half-turned in the direction of his fleeing partner, then folded, neat and silent, before dropping to the ground.

Jed looked down at the man. In the grimace of the 'breed's dying, Jed saw the faint gleam from a gold tooth. He poked his toe at the body and murmured thoughtfully. 'Stupid kid. I was nothing to you. You should have stayed behind.'

To trail him 150 miles, just to pay off a bar-room grudge? And to die for it? It didn't make sense. There had to be more to it than that. Still, Jed thought it unlikely Scranton would return, or the man who'd been standing off, the one who'd mentioned his name. Gripping his gun, Jed took a lingering look into the darkness. He listened for the slightest sound, but whoever'd been out there was way gone.

It was instinct and the continuing silence that made Jed turn towards his horse. Instead of firing wildly, the young 'breed had thought about Jed's pursuit. The Appaloosa was dead. There was a dark, viscous rill across its neck, and its limbs twitched as it died, its head stretched along the blood-soaked ground.

Jed stared at the body of his horse in bitter anger; thought on how he should have taken both men, back in Chimney Point. He'd have to make it on foot; buy another horse at San Angelo. It was a hell of a way toting a saddle and traps. The man called Buck would be paying for it one day; the son-of-a-bitch who'd made mention of the Crane family.

He pounded his Walker Colt into the palm of his hand. One wham from the barrel was usually enough for a man, two would fell a mule if Jed put some meat behind it. From fifty feet, its .44 bullet could take away an arm. It was a bad mistake to have killed his horse, but an even bigger one to have left him with his gun.

He raised his arm high in the air, eased back the hammer and squeezed the trigger. The crack of the single shot would carry a vast distance. To the ears of those who had run, it proclaimed revenge.

2

Cactus Rose

Sebastian Pinto was emptying a rabbit trap. It was where an arroyo of the Pecos River broke flat and thin as it reached into the plain. Partly screened by the bole of a tupelo, he dropped a lank bundle of grey fur to the ground. He looked along the edge of water and held his battered sombrero against the high sun.

The house stood alongside the barn, a corral with a few fine horses and a ramshack bunkhouse for itinerant *vaqueros*. But it was his house — the *estancia* — he was most proud of. Its adobe walls were three feet thick, and he'd added rooms. The shake roof was laid on two feet of sod, and there were four windows with glass. The old man smiled. He'd made his family comfortable, even through the years with no money or cattle for market.

Sebastian's face was crumpled like the soil, only darker. His eyes were all but black, and he had a stubble of silver hair. He turned to his eldest son, who was hefting a small gunny sack on to his shoulder. He listened patiently, as once again the young man poured out his misgivings.

'How much longer, Pa? How much longer we allow Crane's people to take from us? Soon we'll have nothing.'

'We can go on a while longer,' said Sebastian wearily. 'I know how it is, it's bad, but to fight would bring suffering.'

'Yes, Pa. As well as the shame it's already brought,' Olmedo responded bitterly. 'How much longer do we cringe from the *gringos*? I am not a man to do this.'

Sebastian's eyes wandered across the sun-dried grass. In the evening light, it stretched as far as he could see. It was a good place, he thought, but for how much longer? Olmedo wanted to risk it all for the sake of a few yearlings.

Olmedo was still talking, his dark face burning with anger and frustration. 'These men of Rule's, they're riding for Crane,' he said, unable to control the shake in his voice. 'They treat us like the dirt we spit on.'

'Yes, Olmedo, as you say, they bring shame on us. But once you start, you must carry on.' Sebastian tugged at the brim of his sombrero. 'You forget that Gideon Crane and I were friends at one time.'

'I haven't forgot, Pa, but is it a friend who takes the food from the mouths of your children? Is it a friend who hires gunmen to shoot at those that protest?'

The old man looked sharply at his son. 'I cannot believe that it is him. Not after all these years. I will go and see him. We can talk about it. It's not *your* way, Olmedo, but *I'm* getting too old and tired for a fight.'

Olmedo was impatient and frustrated. 'Going to see him won't help us. Crane doesn't pull the strings at Indian Stone; he's lost it. Rule's taken over. Talking won't get you rat feed.'

Sebastian watched Olmedo stump off towards his horse. He picked up the dead rabbit, and closed his eyes. He wanted to shut off the inevitable. Olmedo was proud, volatile, off on the prod, and he couldn't hold him back. Olmedo would fire up his brothers, and together they'd go up against the Indian Stone crowd. That would be bad for the Pinto family.

★　★　★

Like most Texas cattlemen, Gideon Crane had been scratch poor since The War Between the States. Then, a short while ago, extra men were riding from his Indian Stone ranch. It quickly became known that these men were actually hired by the county sheriff, Buckminster Rule. In effect, Rule was now running the spread. Gideon Crane had become the owner of Indian Stone in name only.

Texas was choking with such lawmen. They were appointed by the federal administration as peacekeepers, but a few — and Buck Rule was one of them — worked too closely with crooked politicians and carpetbaggers.

The new hired hands eagerly rammed an Indian Stone brand on everything that ate grass. Neighbouring stockmen had protested, only to end up bleached bones, miles out on the *llano*.

Sebastian Pinto had suffered his losses too, and in his attempt to avoid further bloodshed, put a curfew on his headstrong boys. He was distressed, because he couldn't understand the change. Before the war, the Cranes got on well enough with all their neighbours.

But the Crane boys were gone. The oldest, Sully, joined the Texas Brigade, and died at Vicksburg a year later. A day after the Appomattox peace treaty was signed, Milo was shot dead for his twenty-dollar cavalry horse. Jed, young and uncontrollable, never came home. Nobody knew what had happened to him.

Since then, old Gideon had turned inward, broken and wrathful; like losing his boys had bent his mind. He could have got help from Sebastian to work the cattle, but he turned against him; turned against everyone. The last and worst blow came when he fell under the wheel of a rolling Tilbury wagon. Both his legs were crushed and paralysed and, consumed with bitterness, he'd confined himself to a wheeled chair ever since. The only person prepared to offer comfort was Rafelena, the niece of his dead wife.

The arrogant, northern victors were plundering at will, but for Buck Rule to personally commandeer a man's ranch, was over the line, even for that regime. It bothered Sebastian. He wondered why Gideon Crane, whose bellicose loyalty had always been to the Southern States, appeared to have given in.

Sebastian Pinto had a gut feeling. He knew it was going to get worse.

* * *

Two days later it did. Manolito Pinto, the youngest of Sebastian's four boys, was off hunting. He was splashing his pony through the bed of a shallow arroyo. He'd been daydreaming, and he stopped suddenly, his senses coming to. Reining in, he stood bare-foot in the wood stirrups to watch and listen. He knew the sounds, and he could see what made them.

Along a stand of willow, two riders crowded a bunch of heifers towards him. Mano heeled his pony forward. The riders were unmoved and apparently unconcerned at his approach. Mano pulled up, twisting the pony sideways across their path. His voice was pitched with callow feeling as he opposed the men.

'Hey, where you go with those beef?' He was agitated and angry when he recognized his father's brand on the heifers. It was the *estancia* family brand of Cactus Rose. But it had been crudely mutilated. On its flank, every heifer now bore the recent crush of Gideon Crane's Indian Stone brand.

Mano knew about the men. The one with long white hair was called Scranton. The other, not much older than Mano himself, was called Lipper Weems. Lipper had a face like a piece of sucked candy, and his hair coiled thick from under his billycock hat. To Lipper Weems, everything and anything was wretchedly amusing.

Weems carried two pistols, bandolero style, and Mano could see Scranton's Winchester in a scabbard. To Mano's challenge, Scranton spat a thin stream of dark juice over his shoulder. He responded coldly.

'What's your interest, you scrawny Mex?' He didn't expect any trouble from the boy who appeared unarmed, except for a small cleaver that dangled from his belt.

Lipper looked sideways at Mano and giggled. 'Why don't you tell him, scrawny Mex?' He giggled again.

By now Mano was getting very nervous. Scranton and Weems were infamous, even among Buckminster Rule's crowd. He was on his own, and started to shake from the dread of close oppression. He lacked the big revolvers and repeating rifles, but he wasn't quite as harmless as Scranton thought. He owned a gun. It was an old, heavy Dragoon Colt, which he'd had hidden ever since his father's imposed curfew. He'd brought it out to shoot a few prairie chickens. It always fired when he wanted it to, provided it was kept clean and dry. But it was still rolled in his poncho behind his saddle. He stared wide-eyed in torment, saw the crude grin of Weems, the pale, merciless eyes of Scranton.

'They're not your beef. You turn them loose. They're Cactus Rose brand,' Mano croaked. As he spoke, he grappled behind him for the butt of the Colt.

Harmonied by Weems's high-pitched sniggering, Scranton rasped from deep in his throat. 'They *was* maybe. Now they're Indian Stone.'

As Mano dragged out the Colt, Scranton shot him. The pony snapped away, and for a moment Mano continued his useless grab for the gun. He fumbled with his right hand, while his left clutched the thrashing reins of his pony.

As he fell sideways, his foot caught in his stirrup. Scranton watched cold and impassive, as the boy cried out, his body twisting and turning into the stream. Mano's body trailed for a yard or two, until his foot tore from the stirrup. He convulsed, then lay prone in the shallow arroyo like a bundle of beaten washing. He lay silent, hardly breathing, the side of his face resting on a smooth flat boulder. He just heard the singing of the gnats as they raced above the surface of the water. Then he died, as a water spider sculled a route through the clinch of his thin fingers.

Scranton shoved his Winchester back into its scabbard. 'Courageous little fella, but a tad stupid, don't ya think? What the hell did he think he was gonna do with that heap of old junk, Lipper?'

'Shoot you, Lepe,' Weems replied. He giggled, and saliva trickled down his chin. He gaped at Mano's body. 'What we gonna do with him? Dump him in the *llano* with the others?'

Scranton gave a scornful grunt, and jerked back on the reins of his big roan. 'Leave him lie,' he said. 'Leave him to the fish.'

Weems stared after Scranton. 'There ain't no fishes in there, Lepe,' he said, scratching his head through his hat. He stayed to the rear of Scranton, mumbling, waving the heifers away from the arroyo, not bothering to look back.

3

The Sheriff of Juno Flats

It was early dark, and Jed Crane was within a quarter-mile of Juno Flats. It had been a long day's ride from San Angelo, where he'd helped himself to trapper stew, and an overpriced dun mare. He made a cautious advance on the broken ribbons of light, circuiting to the north, and lying close to the flat banks of the Pecos. The town didn't appear to have changed much since his youth. The river still looped around it, as if by will and wisdom, keeping distance. The water was beginning to widen, harvesting strength in its journey towards an encounter with the Rio Grande. Only in places did it touch the outskirts.

He could see oil lamps in windows of the buildings. He led the mare through the short, furrowed alleys, moving warily until he reached the spine of the main street. He stood amongst the garbage of the shanties, and listened to the town's nightfall. He watched a group of dishevelled uniformed men saunter noisily across the street.

So they were here too, he thought. Yankee officers and ordinary soldiers who'd never given up their killing ways. Like many other towns in Texas, they'd made Juno Flats their centre of operations. At best, they protected the carpetbaggers, speculators and swindlers who came for the pickings. At worst, they lived off their wits, claiming everything for themselves.

His horse faltered momentarily as a small boy raced too close. Jed smiled coldly as the youngster dragged a live cottonmouth through the dust. It was tied by its tail to a long length of string, and he had a friend running behind, lashing its writhing body with a thick switch of willow. Jed shivered, and made gentle, encouraging noises as they walked on.

Wickett's Saloon entertained its small, regular trade of drinkers and drifters. Outside, there was a stocky Mexican hobbling on the ground. He was wresting the lower half of his long-johns with one hand, and waving a small straw hat in the other. He was calling mercies, insistently and plaintively, to a half-naked woman. '*Qué pasa Maria, qué pasa?*' She was wearing loose woolly drawers and jemmy boots. She called out, '*bastardo burro*', and staggered drunkenly up the steps of the saloon.

A seasoned *vaquero* stood on the boardwalk talking to himself. Every now and again he dropped scraps of dry meat at a snuffling dog that crouched in the street below. From inside, someone and a piano struggled with the tune of 'Dancin' Britches'.

Jed walked the mare up to the saloon's hitching post, and glanced along the line to a chestnut gelding, standing quietly at the end. In front of him, a cowboy sat in a chair with his legs propped on the low railing. His Stetson was pulled down low across his face, but he was watching the street. He raised his head slightly as Jed stepped up beside him. 'Evenin',' he said tentatively.

Jed nodded and looked back at the cowboy. 'If you've been sittin' there awhile, you'll know who rode in on the gelding.'

There was a pause, and the cowboy let his feet drop to the ground. 'I guess you recognize the brand.' The man pushed back his Stetson. 'Figured you'd turn up one day, Crane.'

Jed was startled. It was the second time his name had been used. 'Yeah, well, you got that right, fella. But I was askin' after who rides the gelding.'

The cowboy answered slowly, and with a touch of concern. 'The man's name is Buckminster Rule.' He eyed Jed carefully. 'You'll find him inside. I wouldn't push him for a bill of sale though. He's with his friends.'

'What difference does that make?'

The cowboy gave a muffled snort. 'The difference *is*, he's the law. He's the Sheriff of Langtry County, and those friends include army, businessmen and his deputy.'

'I'll wait here,' said Jed. Suddenly he looked more closely at the cowboy. 'If you know who I am, you'll know if there are any friends of *mine* hereabouts?'

This time the cowboy laughed. 'From what I recall, you never had any. If you did, they're probably dead.'

The cowboy's response had no outward effect on Jed; he was momentarily deep in thought. Then he ticked a finger at the cowboy. 'You're Billy Newton?'

'That's right,' said Newton. 'An' if you know what's good for you, Jed Crane, you'll ride on.'

Jed grinned agreeably. 'Can't rightly do that just yet. Not until I've found out why this man's riding a horse with the Crane brand smacked across its rump.'

Newton shrugged, and eased himself up from his chair. He was wearing ill-fitting denims, high boots, and had a Le Mat revolver tucked into a broad leather belt. He grinned back at Jed, and said derisively, 'Could be it's bought and paid for. But then again —?'

That was when the saloon doors flew open, and two men came out. One of them wore a faded trooper's uniform. As they stepped down into the street, their faces were shadowed by their hats. The army man carried an army-issue Colt, holstered high around his waist, the ragged stripes of a corporal hanging from his arm. For a moment the men stood talking, and they didn't notice Jed moving along the boardwalk.

Buckminster Rule was a big man, in a black suit. His hat was pulled tight over a shiny, hairless skull.

'Sheriff,' Jed said, his words flat, but effective. 'If you've a minute, there's something I gotta know.'

Rule was immediately wary, and he

peered up into the shadows of the saloon's low overhang. 'Do I know you, mister?' His practised cunning sensed danger, and he moved sideways away from his colleague, ready to outflank Jed. 'Who the hell are you?' He shifted his eyes to Billy Newton.

Jed chilled at the sound of Buckminster Rule's low voice.

'Jed Crane,' Newton cut in, to Rule's fierce question. 'Gideon's boy. He's come back.'

For reasons of purpose or caution, the sheriff's aide hadn't moved away, and Rule himself wasn't alarmed at Jed's confrontation. The big man spoke crudely. 'Seems I've heard the name. Whoever you are, boy, you start any trouble here an' you won't live to finish it. This corporal o' mine mayn't look much, but he'll shoot ya where ya stand if he has to.'

Rule wasn't daft; he'd seen the movement of Jed's hand. He was doing Jed's thinking for him.

Jed had been considering the possibility of a fight when Newton moved in behind him. He knew that even with an edge of two, or three to one, Rule couldn't be that sure, unless he'd the stand advantage. And Rule knew it too. He'd be the first to die, if Jed pulled the Walker Colt.

The brief impasse was interrupted when Billy Newton pushed in with his sharp warning. 'Don't do it, Jed. I can't miss from where I'm standing.'

Billy was Rule's advantage, and he was holding the grapeshot revolver. A small smile broke across his face. 'Sorry, Jed, you shoulda thought it out.'

'You'd never have tried that facing me,' Jed snapped at him.

Newton's smile vanished, and his manner turned dangerous and prickly. 'Don't get too smart, Jed. You're gonna learn the Cranes ain't throwin' their weight around Langtry County any more.'

Rule took off his sweat-stained hat and swiped his hand across the top of his head. 'Up to now, Billy, I wondered if you rightly knew which side to tuck

35

yerself up with.' Then he winked maliciously at Jed. He turned to the man with corporal stripes. 'Take his gun, Turl.'

The man stepped forward and snatched at Jed's Colt. 'What now, Buck?' he asked. The few words carried a whiff of excitement. 'Take him out-a-ways?'

Rule tutted and pursed his lips at the suggestion. 'And introduce him to your friends of the 'Uplift Society'? No, Turl. Can't let Mr Crane think we're not upholding the law.'

Jed wanted to turn on Billy Newton, but he kept his eyes locked on Buck Rule, who was nodding at Turl.

'Take him to the jail. Tell Micah to lock him up. I've just arrested him for murder.'

Turl struck the frame of the Walker Colt against Jed's spine. 'You heard the sheriff, an' you know which way we're headed. Get goin'.'

Jed looked calmly at Rule. 'What about my horse?'

'Someone'll take it down to the livery stable. Belongs to you does it, the mare?'

'You're the one who's ridin' a stolen horse, Sheriff.'

Rule slapped his hat against his leg. 'You'll need to keep a soft bit on that funnin', Crane.'

4

Billy Newton

Gideon Crane sat stony-faced in his wheeled chair. His hair was thin, loose and unkempt and his spiky brows clutched the tops of his sunken eyes as he scowled at the girl. His bony hands were clenched, resting on the lap-rug stretched tight across his knees.

Through a window, Rafelena was watching the men in the ranch enclosure. She turned and spoke to the old man, her voice flat and cheerless. 'Can you see something in those men that I can't? What is it? Why do you have them around, Gideon?'

'I don't see anything in them, because I can't. Not from here. I don't have much of a choice,' he said harshly. 'They have the advantage of not being overseen, in case you hadn't noticed.'

Rafelena bit her lip. Her positioning was bad. She was caught between Gideon and the cause of his lost holdings, and she moved away from the window.

Gideon looked up at her, then down at his hands. 'They're rubbish and they're trouble, Lena, like you say. But what can I do? I'm sorry.'

Rafelena was his dead wife's niece, and she'd looked after him since his accident. She was small, and had long dark hair. She only wore homespuns; there was no reason for anything else. 'I don't know,' she said kindly, and suddenly smiled. 'One of them came on to me, the other day.'

Gideon glared and raised his fists. 'Came on to you? What does that mean? Which one? Who are you talking about?' He made a grab for his stick, and slammed it against the side of his chair.

The ferocity made Lena start. 'It's all right, Gideon. It wasn't much more than he's tried since I arrived here. I can handle him. If I can't, I'll call you for help.'

Gideon's frustrated misery welled up. 'I can't even look after you properly, can I?'

'I'm supposed to be looking out for you, remember? He was only herding me some.' Rafelena moved towards Gideon. She kneeled on the floor beside him and put her hands over his. 'Don't fear for me, just tell me what they're really doing here.'

Gideon sat for a few moments before he spoke. He was obviously suffering from deep regret. 'It was after the boys had gone. Rule came to see me. He offered to help, and I made a deal with him. I had to try and keep the ranch, Lena.'

Rafelena could see the anguish, as he carried on. 'It was so easy for him, and I didn't see it. He was going to arrange for the cattle to be driven north. There's fat money for beef in Kansas.'

Rafelena looked at him, not under-standing. 'More money than we can make down here, yes. But what happened, Gideon?' She watched as Gideon's jaw trembled.

'He took the money. He still does. It was a good deal for him. The worst for me. We get nothing except . . . ' Gideon's words trailed off.

Rafelena gently broke into his despair. 'So that's what they've been doing. Driving the stock into Oklahoma. To the railhead for Kansas?'

'Yes, Lena, now you know. There's not much left. Buck Rule'll suck the blood out of the ranch until there's nothing left. He'll be moving on the house next.'

He stared bleakly around the room, heeding the loss of everything. As if he'd forgotten Lena, he stumbled on, 'If I had the boys . . . but on my own . . . a dumped cripple.'

Rafelena went back to look out the window. 'Don't let go yet, Gideon. There'll be a way out.' She turned to face him. 'Why not get someone else to take a herd to Chimney Point?'

'Someone else,' he snarled. 'There's no someone else. They're all as bad as each other. Even them long-time neighbourly Pintos have been stringing my heifers down to El Paso.'

'You've no proof of that Gideon. Your mind's been poisoned,' Rafelena objected.

Since Milo, his second son, had been killed, Gideon had suffered these dark bouts. Rafelena wondered whether she herself was getting beyond his regard and trust.

'Why don't you ask Billy Newton? He's honest, isn't he?'

'Billy Newton? I know you mean well, gal, but no. There's no way out. I'm finished.'

Rafelena rubbed her hands across her face, smearing tears. There wasn't much point in discussing or encouraging, she'd have to come up with something herself. She didn't know how far Gideon's mind had run amok, but there was no question of Buckminster Rule's contribution. She wouldn't quit on him though, regardless of any danger to herself. They could still fight.

★ ★ ★

It was approaching full dark as Buck Rule watched his deputy push Jed Crane down the street. 'That'll close him up a bit,' he said, his heavy body rolling with indulgence. He narrowed his eyes at Billy Newton. 'Maybe I had you pegged out wrong, Billy. I was thinkin' you and him was close at one time.'

Newton shrugged. 'I knew him, but not close. I had an understanding with his brother. They were just sappy schemes, though.'

'You know there's work for a man like you, Billy. There's money to be made, and I'm thinkin' favourably on it. Stick around for a while.' Rule clapped a big hand on Newton's shoulder.

They stood outside the saloon, until they were joined by Danton Cheever, a lumber merchant, and Buffer Wagnall, the small, red-faced man who owned the dry-goods and hardware store. Wagnall was unsteady on his feet because he'd been drinking all evening.

He said thickly, 'I do so like the dark, gentlemen. It sort of evens things out. Nothing seems quite as bad.'

Rule shot a glance at Cheever, who simply shrugged his shoulders.

Wagnall continued, 'Well, gentlemen, we can't stand around here all night. Join me for supper.'

Again, Rule looked questioningly at Cheever. But Wagnall understood, and said more directly, 'I'll guarantee my supper's a tad up on the swill we've been paying for in there.' Wagnall rolled his eyes at the prospect. 'If you follow me, I can offer you better, in private.'

'Yes, thank you, Buffer,' Rule said. 'The town seems peaceable enough. And as I'm the only one likely to cause trouble . . . ' He laughed deep and meaningfully at his observation.

The three men walked across the street. Billy Newton was hesitant behind them, but Rule turned and waved him forward.

Lamps were burning in Wagnall's store, and an assistant edged subserviently past them as they pushed in. Wagnall ignored him, other than to accept a large bunch of keys as they passed in the doorway. He led the men to the back of the store, through stacked flour bags, barrels and digging tools. He stumbled against the end of his packed counter, before fumbling a key into the door of his store-room and office.

'Come in, gentlemen. It's not only the finest quality bullets and nails that I stock,' he said intimately.

The room was a clutter of frontier commodities. Everything from tinned peaches and horehound candy to bucksaws and axe heads. In the corner were two chairs and a narrow davenport. Wagnall eased himself down full-length, and pointed to a small cupboard above his head. 'It's in here, gentlemen. Please help yourself. I fear the evening has the better of me.' He clamped his pink hands across his chest, and within moments, he was snoring, loud and raw.

Buck Rule inspected the bottle he took down from Wagnall's cupboard. 'Well, he was right about the mark of his whiskey. Double-rectified, old corn.'

Billy Newton stood uncomfortably, hoping it deceived Rule. He wondered why the sheriff had wanted him along, but accepted his share of the good whiskey.

'He won't be hearing much for a while,' Rule said, looking down at Wagnall. He sat heavily in one of the chairs, and nodded for Newton to sit catercorner at the table. Cheever remained standing, a knowing smirk across his face.

Rule held up his glass. 'We'll drink to your attachment, Billy.' But there's a question of, er . . . loyalty.' Rule looked cagily at Newton.

'I can be loyal. Do you want

something of me?' Newton asked doubtfully.

Rule topped up their glasses. 'Yeah, there *is* something, Billy. The sheriff drew a short-barrelled, single-action revolver, that he'd been carrying in his frock coat. He placed it in front of Newton, and smiled. 'It's about that man, Crane. We don't need him turnin' up here, do we?'

Newton put his glass on the table, and stared at the gun. 'You want me to kill him? Is that the 'something' you're talking about?' He glanced at Cheever, looking and sounding suitably shocked.

Rule chortled, and shook his head slowly. 'No, no, no, Billy. How could I ask you to do that? I was put here as an officer of the law, remember.'

Wagnall snored contentedly. There wasn't much doubt of his involvement in any profitable scheming, but he was well out of the discussion.

The sheriff thumbed the cylinder from the pistol. He looked up as he ejected each charge. 'Now listen up,

Billy. Here's what we'd like you to do.'

As he explained — carefully leaving the percussion caps in position — his expression became more serious. Cheever took advantage of the corn whiskey, as Billy Newton's predicament came clear.

5

The Set-Up

The graffiti-covered, mud-faced walls shimmered in the light from the lamp that hung outside the door of Jed's cell. He looked around him gloomily; a litter-bed against one wall, a barred window and a dirt-can. The fermenting whiff stung his eyes and the back of his throat. According to the sheriff, he'd been jailed for murder.

It was Buckminster Rule who had stayed back, the night they'd tried to shoot him up at his night camp. It was Rule who had mentioned the Crane name. That's why they'd dogged him all the way from Chimney Point. Rule must have been there, with Scranton. But they'd also been on the return to Juno Flats. Jed had walked under the evil star. He'd been guilty before he pulled up at Wickett's Saloon.

He couldn't understand Rule indicting him for killing the half-breed. It happened nearly fifty miles outside the Texas border. But then again, it seemed that Rule was more than law in Juno Flats, or Langtry County. It was Rule's own law, wherever it stretched, and whatever he said it was. Jed knew the sheriff wasn't thinking of a trial. His deputy, Turl O'Brien, certainly wasn't. He'd be for the nearest tree, and a jerking to Jesus. With some conviction, Jed knew Rule was going to keep an advantage; stay ahead until something else occurred to him.

He hunched down with his back against the cell door, facing the window. It was a tangle. He knew his father had to be involved. Rule was on the hop, because Jed's last name was Crane, not because he'd killed the half-breed, or because of his run-in with Scranton.

Scranton must have recognized him

from the federal prison pen at Galesburg; remembered his name; made a link with Indian Stone ranch. But he couldn't have been certain. Whatever was going on, Rule had wanted Jed out of the way, just in case there was a family connection. That's what worried Jed. What was it, that made it necessary to kill him?

It was something to do with the ranch. Rule was even riding a horse with an Indian Stone brand. Jed's heart thumped with helpless anxiety. There was something wrong out at the ranch.

Since he'd ridden off to join the army, there'd been no contact between Jed and his father, or his brothers. Maybe they'd known of his capture, but a message or letter never came through. And he hadn't written home; too ashamed after the rout at Stones River. Since the Galesburg Pen, the in-between years hadn't changed much. His egg in whiskey, at the Silver Ribbon, had confirmed that.

Jed had to stop his mind racing; turn

his thoughts to something more practical. He'd been coming home anyway; he'd have found out. Meeting Scranton wasn't bad luck or timing, it was fate.

He unbent from his crouched position, and stepped over to the window. The moon was in its first quarter, and the sky was turning from deep grey to black. By pushing the side of his face hard against the bars, he could just see where the alley bent around the jail. At the corner, in the yellow light of an open doorway, there was an old man humming a tune, then singing. Jed squinted to see the other way, but that end of the alley was too dark to reveal anything. He could hear some of the man's song, He'd heard it before, hundreds of miles to the east; Pea River? Or maybe it was Galesburg.

Jed stopped the memory as a nosing rat scuttled across the dirt floor. He shuddered, then backed off from the window. His stomach had started to churn. The jail was set well back from the main street, trapped in the pungency of animal fur, stable dust and canhouse swill.

He knew the geography well enough. There were corrals behind the livery barn, and a run of stocksheds; then open land, straight to the rim of the Edwards Plateau. He'd have to come up with something.

He stared at the shaky frame of the litter. In the Galesburg Pen, he'd found a spoon. He'd broken off the bowl, and sharpened the handle on a stone to fashion a mean weapon. A vague and fleeting memory of a Yankee guard returned, and Jed kicked at the litter reckless and angry, as he thought back. Billy Newton. What was his problem? He'd talked real nice. Then he'd pulled that grapeshot revolver and offered Jed to the sheriff. Jed's face twisted into a grimace. Perhaps the deception was worthy of a little admiration, but if Jed got hold of him . . .

He lay, troubled and weary, on the broken litter. Why had Billy done that?

They'd got along well enough growing up, even though Billy had been more of a friend to his brother, Milo. Now it had all changed, and Billy Newton was running with the opposition.

★ ★ ★

It was an hour later that the sound woke him. His nerves tightened when across the bars of the small window, a face appeared. It was darkly silhouetted against the black sky. His muscles seized with fear. He'd been dreaming that outside Wickett's Saloon, Turl O'Brien had wanted to take him away and lynch him.

Reality snapped him from the chimera of wearied sleep. Rule had ordered him to be thrown in jail, but had he changed his mind? Sent someone from that 'Uplift Society'?

Jed pushed himself up and away from the litter. He moved to the far wall, standing still and helpless as the low whispers reached into the cell.

'Jed, you in there? Come over here.'
It was the voice of Billy Newton.

Jed shivered involuntarily from the icy sweat that ran between his shoulder blades. If Newton meant to shoot him, there wasn't a lot he could do about it. He could die toughing it out though. 'Found another safe place, Newton? All I've got is a piss-pot, this time.'

'Listen up Crane, I don't have much time. Take hold o' this. I don't want to drop it.'

Jed stared, as Newton thrust his hand through the window bars. He was holding a short-barrelled revolver. Jed didn't move. If he went forward, Newton could turn the gun and shoot him. From that close-up he wouldn't miss, even in the dark. His nerves jumped violently.

'Didn't figure on me being in here, and still alive, did you, Newton?' he said, his nerves still jumping.

'For Chris'sake, Jed, listen to me. You're in trouble, and only seeing the narrow picture.' He moved, and Jed could see the thinnest of lamp-light across his face. Jed sidled further into the corner of the cell, as Newton continued. 'I know what you're thinking, how it looks. But just think about it for a second. If it hadn't been for me, there'd be someone knocking pine planks around you right now. You think you could have taken out the Sheriff and his deputy?'

'You should have given me the chance to find out. What was my life to you?'

'I don't have time to argue with you, Jed, take the gun. You do what I say, and maybe you'll get out of here. Maybe even stay alive. It's up to you.'

Jed stayed where he was. 'Say what you've got to. I can't do much else but listen.'

'It's a set-up. I'm to get the gun to you, primed, but not loaded. Old Micah checks you out before he turns in. When he does . . . well, the rest's up to you.'

'Yeah, and what if this Micah knows

about it? Then what? A goodnight kiss from the barrel of his shotgun?'

'You're still not thinkin', Jed. He doesn't know. You're supposed to get out.'

'What happens when I get out? That's when he shoots me?'

'No. You'll run straight into a couple o' so-called deputies. They'll shoot you.'

'You must have something else in mind, Newton. That little scene ain't too encouraging.'

'Take the gun, Jed. Have a look. I've reloaded it. Just take it. I can't stay around here any longer.'

Jed tried quickly to sort it out. If he could get his hands on the gun, and it *was* loaded and primed, he'd have nothing to lose; unless there was something he hadn't thought on. But that was the chance he'd have to take.

'Leave it on the ledge,' he said, a shade uneasily. He didn't know whether it was a short cut to the town's Boot Hill, but at least he'd have a gun.

He watched closely, as Newton

placed the gun between the bars, across the thick ledge. He decided he'd give one more person, one more chance. 'If it's all right with you, I'll leave the thankin' for later on.'

'Don't forget the two deputies. I'll get to you with a horse, out beyond the corrals,' Newton told him. 'We'll both have to take leave of this town,' he said finally, dropping back to the alley.

6

The Breakout

Jed left it ten minutes before he made a move for the gun. He checked it and, sure enough, it was in firing order. He sat on the floor, his head in his hands. There was a lot happening, and he knew none of it. Even if Billy Newton was on the level, his allegiance to Jed was a shaky one. Jed's immediate future was grim, either side of the cell wall.

Newton had said that Rule's deputies would 'take him' when he walked from the jail. He held a loaded gun now, but the killers would have a big advantage. He'd have to change the rules.

The jailer checked on him before midnight, but Jed didn't attempt his breakout. It was a way of testing Newton's intent, his standpoint. Jed was still worried about the jailer and,

59

after he'd gone, he lay awake for nearly four hours. No one visited the jail, and Jed ceded that the man hadn't been privvy to Rule's arrangement. He'd make his move at first light; make the deputies wait for their treacherous work. He'd give himself the edge of surprise, and a couple of hours' faltering rest.

★   ★   ★

It was approaching five, when Jed heard Old Micah stomping around in the front office of the jail. There was the drift of coffee, and his uneasy stomach could look forward to pone, and maybe something in a bowl.

He'd force himself to be patient, get some sustenance, before he made his move. He was standing with his hands against the bars when Old Micah brought through the early meal.

'What do you do all day, old man? With only me to look after, you must get real bored.'

Micah pushed through the coffee and meagre food. 'Play checkers with meself,' he said curtly. 'What's it to you?'

'Nothin', I just wondered. Envious, I guess.'

The old jailer looked into the cell. 'What's your bed doin' stood up over there?'

Jed looked at the litter he'd propped against the wall beside the window. 'It's broken. Anyway, it gives me more room. I don't like confined spaces.'

'Well, put it back. I don't like it there,' Micah said. 'Put it back where it should be, else I won't take out yer dirt-pail.'

'Yessir. I'll see to it when I've finished my breakfast.' Jed responded quietly, as Micah wandered back to the office.

He made short work of the food, then tucked Newton's gun into the front of his pants. He pulled the litter from the wall, and slammed it hard down on to the floor. He yelled loudly, then quickly wedged himself beneath the shattered slats.

Within moments, Micah was peering through the bars. 'What the hell you done? Can you hear me, Crane?' He hurried back for the keys to the cell. 'Lordamighty, what's the boy done?' he muttered, with the rub of genuine concern.

Jed slid the gun between his chest and the underside of the litter, closed his eyes and waited for Micah.

Micah was gibbering as he twisted the cell keys and pushed open the door. He stooped towards Jed who was lying still and silent beneath the litter. 'You ain't killed yerself have you, boy?' he quavered.

'No,' Jed said, smiling broadly up into the old man's worried face. He eased out the gun, and aimed it at Micah's stomach. 'Pull this crate off me.'

Micah seemed more relieved than frightened, as he eased the litter clear of Jed. 'You had me real worried there for a while.'

Jed got to his feet, and nodded. 'Thanks. Where's your shotgun?'

'I didn't think I'd need it,' Micah said. 'It's in the gun rack. Why? You ain't gonna shoot me, are yer, boy? I done you no harm.'

'I know you haven't, and I ain't gonna shoot yer. Just keep quiet.'

Micah held up his shaking hands. 'I will. I been doin' that for longer'n I can remember.'

Jed stared at him for a few seconds. 'Good. I'm not even going to lock you up. But you'll be staying here, and you won't even make the sound of a sick mouse. Stay here, until the sheriff arrives.'

Jed stood outside the cell and looked toward the office. 'Have you got my gun out there? The big Walker?'

Micah just pointed.

Crane narrowed his eyes. 'Remember, if you do anything before then, I'll come back and do something real bad to you.'

Knowing the jailer was too frightened

to move, Jed walked to the office. A big, steaming mug of coffee stood in the middle of Micah's well-used checker board, and the door of the gun rack sagged open above a desk. He grunted with approval as he caught sight of his own gun lying under a sheaf of Wanted posters. He removed the cylinder from Newton's gun, and tossed the frame on to the desk. He checked the cylinder and caps of his Colt, and gripped the butt reassuringly. With his left hand, he reached into the rack and took Micah's shotgun.

His muscles were tense and he was sweating a little, as he edged out of the jail. He took a few deep breaths, and looked around him uneasily. He backed into the alley that sided the jail, and paused again to listen. There was no yelling, and nobody shot at him; only a rooster crowed in the distance.

Carrying two guns, he sidled towards the rear of the jail. He stopped at the end of the alley, and quartered the ground ahead. He saw a cluster of sheds to his left, and ahead of him, the corral which held a lone horse. Beyond that, the open range, crushed and colourless, under the flat, early light.

He moved into the lee of the sheds. The horse was fractious, and he watched as it raised its head, flick-eared, towards the street side of the corral, the side nearest the jail. Jed leaned the shotgun carefully against the wall of the shed, and stepped out.

Outlined against the yellow glow from the east, he'd seen the men he wanted. They were close together, talking quietly, paid to be waiting. Both were wearing army-issue pants, and carrying sidearms. There was no mis-take in their identity, only in them being there.

'You two,' he called. 'Waiting for me?'

The two deputies looked at each other in sudden alarm. One of them recovered quickly and glared towards Jed. 'You took your time, mister,' he barked. 'We been numbin' ourselves out here.'

The smaller of the two idled sideways, laughing. He nodded at the gun in Jed's hand. 'How dya wanna play it, Crane? You gonna throw that thing at us first, or after you've pulled the trigger?'

Jed gave a genuine smile. He could hardly believe it. 'No, you've got it all wrong. Take a close look at the gun.' His head scarcely moved in the direction of his hand. 'Not quite what you were expectin', you murderin' trash. This is a .44 Walker Colt. I returned it to me, on the way out.'

The deputies' faces flicked back and forth, between the gun and Jed's face. They paled, and their bodies tensed. They wanted to look at each other, but dared not take their eyes off Jed.

Jed almost hissed at them, 'Now, how do you want to play it?'

His gut hardened, and he slowly lowered the big Colt to his side. The ruthless bullies would have shot him dead, unarmed and defenceless. He waited for a sign of movement, but it wasn't possible to keep his concentration on both; they were just too far spread.

That's what they were relying on. There was a thin, taunting sneer from the man on the left, but Jed didn't flinch. There was no other way now, and he knew it would be the small one who'd shoot first.

The irked horse slammed its hooves into the poles of the low corral, and Jed knew it was the moment. He caught the small one grabbing for his holster.

Before the barrel had cleared leather, Jed's wrist was bucking, as he thumbed back the hammer of his Colt. The man jerked back as the bullet struck him in the chest. He was lifted up on his toes, as if trying to appear taller, then he pitched forward, slamming into the hard-packed dirt. Jed watched as the man's hand dragged again at his gun, but it was over, and the body finally caved in. He stepped forward to the lifeless deputy. He looked at the dead face, then back at the second man who was standing rooted to the spot.

He gaped with foreboding at Jed. 'Not me, mister. I'm not sworn in, never was. I'm just wearin' the badge. It don't mean nothin'.'

'It should: it's just cost you your life.' Jed pulled back the hammer for the second time.

The man had to make a try to live, and he made a futile grab for his own Colt. Jed waited for him to level the gun, and he shook his head as the doomed man palmed the hammer with his other hand. Jed's bullet caught him in the left shoulder, spinning him round with the impact. Clutching his gun in both hands, the man managed to fire one shot that ploughed into the ground between his buckling legs. Jed fired again, and the man crashed back against the corral. He hung there for several seconds, then fell, throwing his gun out ahead of him.

Jed pushed the .44 beneath his buckskin coat. 'Don't know how much Rules paid you men for this, but it wasn't enough,' he muttered.

There was movement behind him, in the shadows. Two or three people had already appeared, and Jed looked at their indolent faces, as if encouraging a reprisal, but they didn't seem to know what to do, or appear to care. As he moved off, a mangy grey dog sprang from the corral and snapped viciously at his heels. He looked directly into the spiteful yellow eyes, and instinctively moved his hand back to his Colt. Then, from beyond the stock-sheds, a voice yelled, short and urgent.

'Ben, leave it. Get over here.'

The man was wearing ill-fitting clothes and wore high boots. He led an Indian Stone horse, the chestnut gelding Jed had seen tied outside Wickett's Saloon. Jed took the reins and climbed eagerly into the saddle. 'You're full of surprises, Billy,' he said, as he swung the horse around. 'An' you have a lot of explaining to do. We'll ride north.'

7

The Bad Years

They took to the plain, scattering rabbits and quail from their mesquite hiding. They maintained an easy pace, and kept to the contours of the Pecos as it wound up to the foothills. Every hour they allowed the horses a drink and kickstomp where the water shallowed. They rode until they were fifty miles north-east of Juno Flats. The land threw deep, orange light into their faces, and the distant Glass Mountains stood black and dark against the disappearing sun.

They stopped and stood alone, listening to the sounds of their own heavy breathing, and the soft twitterings of small birds at roost in the scrub. There was young clover and snake bunny in the summer grasses where the men dismounted. The muscles of Jed's gelding were quivering, and its coat glistened in the darkness as it pawed the earth in anticipation. Billy Newton had brought supplies, and they feasted off jack-rabbit and beans, onions and corn bread.

An hour later, Jed made himself easy, his back firmly bolstered in the curve of his saddle. He drew a blanket around him, laid his head back, and looked up into the inky-blue darkness.

'Listen to me, Billy Newton,' he said. 'In the last few days, I've had to shoot at half-a-dozen men. Three of them are dead. Now you tell me why.'

'You've been gone a long time, Jed, and what's happened ain't good. And in case you're still wonderin', Rule would have had those deputies put bullets in me. I knew too much. I owe you for that.'

'That's as maybe, Billy. I want to know the rest.'

Billy tossed the dregs of his coffee into the small fire. 'I'll give you the rest,

Jed, but you ain't gonna like it.' He cleared his throat. 'Your brother, Sully, was killed at Vicksburg. Milo made it through safely, but . . . ' Billy's voice faltered. 'Then he met up with a group of Rule's men.'

A short silence followed before Jed spoke. 'What happened, Billy?'

'They stopped him outside Cheever's Store. It was late, they'd been inside drinking, and they wanted his horse. It was only one of your old man's cow ponies. Milo could have talked himself out of it. He would've only gone for his gun to scare 'em off. He ought to have had more sense. One of 'em shot him out of the saddle.'

'Who were they?'

'Lipper Weems was one of 'em. The one who rode off with the horse. Remember Chum Weems, over at Teal Creek? Lipper's his oldest.'

'Yeah, I remember 'em. Lipper was no more'n a kid. An ugly little runt from what I remember. Was it him shot Milo?'

'No, that was Scranton. Lepe Scranton.'

'Scranton?' Jed repeated. 'What's he look like?'

'Tall, long white hair, mangy. Why? You know him?'

'We've met, but I never knew his name,' Jed said thoughtfully.

He told Billy about the confrontation at Chimney Point, and about Scranton and the half-breed coming at him later. 'Scranton was a patrol guard at Galesburg. It was Buck Rule who mentioned my name. I still don't know what the hell he was talking about, Billy. I hope you're going to tell me.'

Billy was suddenly surprised and curious. 'You were at Galesburg? That was a prisoner o' war camp. How'd you get in there?'

'It's a long story. Not for the tellin' now.'

'Christ, you know how to fuse trouble, Jed. The 'breed you killed, was Gato March. He saw himself as kin to Scranton.'

Jed was unmoved. He stared at the last of the fire's embers as they crackled and glittered. 'Buckminster Rule, Billy. Why was he ridin' the Indian Stone horse? Other than it being a fine ride. You never did answer me that.'

Billy was uneasy, and his reply was hesitant. 'It seems like he's some influence on your old man . . . got him in his clutches . . . that's what some are sayin', Jed. Even got his eye on the girl, apparently.'

'What girl?' Jed asked.

Billy thought for a second. 'A bit after your time,' he said. 'Rafelena's her name. Her mother brought her all the way from Atlanta in '64. They were refugees. I think Mrs Pippin was your ma's sister.'

Jed's own mother had been dead a long time, but he thought he remembered the name of her sister: Mrs Pippin was Jed's aunt. The girl meant nothing to him, but he was stunned at what Billy had to say about his father, that Rule had a hold over him. What could have happened? Gideon Crane always took 'point', and never kow-towed to anyone.

'There's something very wrong, Billy.' Jed felt the agitation of guilt creeping through him.

'Yeah. He certainly hit a dry lode, Jed. He was left with Rafelena when Mrs Pippin was taken with a bad fever. Maybe that was all right though; she's looked after him since. He calls her Lena. She was there when the wagon hit him. It busted him up bad. He ain't done much since.'

Jed pulled his Stetson over his face. For all the hardbark on him, his jaw twitched with emotion; knowing they'd suffered just by him not being there. After Galesburg, he should have come home. He didn't know of his dead brothers, or his father's accident, but he could still give himself a hard time over it.

'Buckminster Rule,' he said slowly. 'Where does he come from?'

'Don't know. Up north somewhere.

He was put into Juno Flats by the administrators.'

'And for a grain of flavouring, he moved in on Indian Stone,' Jed snapped bitterly.

'I think so, Jed. Your old man ain't up to opposing him. Not the way he is now. All that happened, bent his mind. He don't trust nobody.'

'Did he trust Rule?'

'At the beginning maybe. I don't rightly know. He don't get out, I know that much. He's only got Lena.' Billy stopped for a moment. 'That's the problem Rule's got with you, Jed. After all this time . . . just turnin' up.'

Jed lay very still. The silence was affecting, but Billy decided to carry on.

'Rule's men are ridin' roughshod. They're sticking their own mark on all livestock. They're goin' across the range, an' it don't matter what they steal and plunder. Everyone's sufferin'. There's no one to stop 'em, Jed. Maybe if . . .'

Billy went quiet, recognizing the

impact of his telling, but after a few minutes of intense silence, he asked tentatively, 'What you gonna do, Jed?'

'First off, get me some sleep.'

★   ★   ★

In the early morning, they woke to the fresh, biting cold. Spread below them was the Edwards Plateau, stretching 200 miles to the Colorado River. Jed's horse was standing near, watching him, its head bathed in a cloud of spiralling steam. Between dusk and dawn, there were sharp temperature swings in the low foothills. They didn't retain the diffused warmth of the range, or the spiked frost of the high peaks. Jed fixed a short riata and cantered the horse around the withered remains of the camp-fire to stir their circulation and taut muscle.

Billy had found branchwood, so they could make hot coffee. He looked deliberately at Jed. 'You're going to Indian Stone, aren't you?'

Jed nodded. 'As far as I know, the ranch still belongs to the Crane family, and that includes me. About time I did something about it.'

'You'll need help, Jed. Guess I'll tag along.'

Jed grinned wryly. 'This ain't anything to do with you, Billy, an' I'm real obliged, but — '

Billy shook his head. 'No, Jed, I'm coming with you. Lookin' out for your old man's the same as lookin' out for all of us. Why don't we just pack up and get goin'?'

It was an hour past daybreak when the two men rode towards Indian Stone ranch.

8

The Herd

It was mid-morning, and the rising sun fell through the raggedy blinds of the sheriff's office in Juno Flats.

Buck Rule's smugness had deserted him, and he slammed his fist on the desk top. He was bloated with anger as he stared across the table. 'How the hell'd they get away?' he fumed.

Harrell Beggs was a Northerner; took turn as top-hand when Lepe Scranton was away. He wore a mix of old army. His face was covered with short stubbly hair, and his eyes squeezed with tension.

'Billy Newton,' he said rapidly. 'Took your horse from the livery. No one to do much about it at that hour. Musta been real late, or real early.'

Rule swore slowly, with every sacred

phrase he could think of. It helped bring his temper under control. 'I should-a known.' There was a dash of crooked smile across his face. 'He suckered me.'

Beggs squinted at Rule. He wanted activity, but he said nothing.

Rule looked back at him, hard and thoughtful. 'Get someone you can trust. Send 'em to Indian Stone. Tell Chum Weems to stay awake. Crane's likely to try and get to his pa.'

Beggs was ready and eager. 'Done. What about me?'

'Find me another horse, goddammit. We'll get out to the herd. An' tell 'em to take guns. They'll be needed.'

Beggs quickly left the office, and Rule gripped the ends of his desk. Newton taking his horse was a bummer. It wouldn't be long before word spread; worth an ironic snigger around the town. Sweat was already soaking his body, as he pulled himself from his chair.

Jed Crane was worse news; he'd

killed two more men. Nothing good had happened since Chimney Point. He remembered the night they'd shot up Crane's camp. He could have died out there himself, instead of Gato March. Rule shuddered, like someone who'd just had their grave walked over.

He thought how close he'd been — still was — to moving in on Indian Stone. He'd got it all worked out. Poor old Gideon Crane was sliding away, his mind in a mess. And then there was Rafelena. He drew breath at the thought of the girl. It was looking like a ready-made, a winner, but now with the arrival of Jed Crane, none of it was such a sure bet.

He heard loud talking, and horses snorting in the street. He grabbed a Winchester and took a box of ammunition from his desk drawer. Jed Crane was on a loose lead, but from now on there was no more slack in Buck Rule's rope.

* * *

Hash Claymore's chuckwagon was wedged in a stand of alder. A twist of smoke climbed from the fire, where he was preparing the usual sowbelly, beans and biscuits. Smells of the cooking drifted to Buck Rule and his men, where they watched from the top of a low rise.

Rule eyed the rope corral that held the small remuda of cow and pack ponies. Clustered in hundreds of small groups, the herd had started to mill across its bed ground.

This was the herd set to be driven to the Chimney Point railhead. Most were Indian Stone, but it was a stock mix. The cowboys hadn't been too careful about brand marks during their rounding-up. The herd was close to a thousand head, Rule figured.

'Let's get down there,' he called.

Followed by Harrell Beggs, Chark Measurer, and Dawson 'Bird' Cutter, he rode down towards the camp.

Claymore was a stove-up wrangler, with arthritis and bent legs that had never healed straight from multiple breakings. He wore a canvas bag apron and an irked expression. He gestured at the big pot hanging from the tailgate. 'There's an inch of the first coffee; crusty, but it's still warm. If you're lookin' for food, it ain't ready yet.'

Rule dismounted and tipped some stewed coffee into a tin mug. He stared at the contents, then at Claymore. 'Can't see Scranton. Where is he?'

'Checkin' the herd, I guess. He don't always tell me his plans,' was the cook's sour response.

'Send a rider. I want him here.' Rule hunkered beside the wheel of the chuckwagon as Claymore despatched a man to the far side of the herd.

Scranton was riding swing, and he left the go-between to cover for him. It took him twenty minutes to get back to the trail camp, where Rule was waiting for him impatiently. He swung his horse into the ropes of the remuda, tossing the reins towards a wrangler.

He was covered in trail dust, and

looked surprised to see Rule. 'What's goin' on, Buck? It's real early for you. Somethin' wrong?'

'Plenty,' Rule growled. 'Jed Crane rode into town last night.'

'Jesus,' Scranton muttered. 'What did he want?'

'He wanted to know who was ridin' one of his horses.' Briefly, Rule outlined what had happened in town. 'I think he'll be wanting more than that now, though.'

Scranton looked dumbfounded. He took off his hat, and ran his fingers through his long white hair. 'Timing,' he said. 'It's all about timing, Buck. Crane couldn't have got it better; just as we move the herd out to Chimney Point.' He gave a half smile to Claymore who was pounding out sourdough.

'You want that we hold up for a while?'

Rule shook his head. 'We can't do that, Lepe. The buyers are wantin' their beef. We're on a promise. No delivery, no pay. But you'll have to leave a man or two behind to go after Crane.'

'Our record's not that great with him, Buck. You shouldn't have let him see daylight, once you'd jailed him. As for Newton, you musta know'd he was a onetime pal of Crane's.'

'Yeah, well, that ain't getting us nowhere,' Rule said. 'Those deputies were meant to take out both of 'em. They paid a lot for not doin' it.'

Under his breath, Scranton muttered something about Rule paying a lot, then he spoke out, to Beggs, Dawson Cutter and Chark Measurer. 'Crane's got to be found, and he could be anywheres from here to the Mexican border.'

'Won't he try and get to see his pa?' Beggs asked.

'Yeah, could be.' Scranton threw a glance at his colleague. 'You done anything about that?'

'Buck thoughta that. I sent a man out to ol' Chummy Weems. Crane'll get a spicy reception if he pokes his nose in there.'

'What happens if he don't? He knows he ain't got free rein around here.'

Rule joined in. 'That's where you come in, Lepe. I want you to take a posse out for him. He's an escaped outlaw; broke jail. He might not be alone. Think you can find him? Bring him in?'

Scranton looked amused. 'It'll be a cold day in Hell when I can't manage the likes of Crane. Yeah, he won't be any trouble.'

'I doubt that,' Rule suggested. He looked enquiringly at Scranton. 'What exactly was it between you and Crane?'

Lepe Scranton's voice suddenly sounded curiously detached. 'I thought you'd ask sooner or later. I was a guard at the Galesburg stockade. This Jed Crane came in with a small band of Reb captives. Our rations were real poor, but theirs was worse, a lot worse. We traded 'em grub, now and then; bacon, salt, the occasional root vegetable, even bones. Their shebangs always smelled o' stew. Anyways, to cut a long story, I made a deal with Crane. I was after selling him a tent pole an' a blanket. I made him pay up front o' course. Only problem was, I didn't have a pole or a blanket. I remember, it was for twenty lousy secesh dollars, but it bought a few drinks.'

'He remembered too, did he?' Rule taunted.

'He sure did. My boys had to peel him off me. He woulda stuck me like a pig, with a little spoon-dagger.'

Rule snorted derisively. 'Can't say I blame him.'

'Yeah, well, he paid for it later. So did I. Latrine duty, then a transfer north to Camp Douglas.'

Nobody said anything for a moment, but there were a few sidelong glances at Scranton.

Rule pulled his hat off, for a rub at his shining scalp. 'I want you to take young Lipper and the boys. Pick up his old man too. That'll give you the most depraved and meanest bunch in

Christendom. Just get Crane. If you have to shoot him, well . . . '

Scranton understood, and he looked confidently at the man giving orders.

The sun was into its afternoon slide, and it almost haloed Rule's large, gleaming skull. He gently patted the neck of Scranton's big roan. 'If he gets away this time, Lepe, you'll probably be lookin' at more than a dose o' latrine duty. Now get outa here.'

9

Indian Stone

Jed Crane and Billy Newton rode determinedly and hard. They made a long loop, keeping to the harder ground, careful not to raise dust. It was late afternoon when they crested a low bluff that overlooked Indian Stone Ranch. Behind them, the peaks of the Glass Mountains rose beckoningly against the western sky. But it wasn't to the west that Jed must turn his face: it was homeward he had to look, towards the house.

They dismounted to ease their horses, and take in the land ahead.

A wide reach of plain lay below them, where grey mesquite, and golden huisache dotted the hard soil. Nestled in a brake of cottonwood, was the livery stable, weathered sheds and low-walled adobe house of the Crane family. The angled sun picked out the buildings, white and stark.

Jed just stared. It was the first time he'd seen his home in years. But he couldn't ride in. As of yesterday, he'd been outlawed. If the so-called law was down there, they could shoot him from the saddle.

'Looks peaceable enough.' Billy was holding his hand up against the dipping sun. 'Don't reckon on it staying like that if we ride in.'

Jed nodded at the suggestion, but he was looking south. 'Take a look there,' he said.

Billy peered out to where a bunch of riders were breaking into file, walking their horses cautiously into the thick mesquite. 'Who the hell are they?' he asked.

'Dunno, we'll have to get nearer,' Jed said.

Billy climbed back into his saddle. 'Sometime, I'll have to get me a spyglass,' he muttered.

They walked down the bluff, then took narrow cuts through the rough chaparral. The scrub was thorny and high. It brushed their legs, and in places they couldn't see further than five or six paces ahead.

After close to an hour of pushing and winding through the dense chaparral, they broke cover. They were near to the house, and Jed gestured for care.

From closer up, neglect was beginning to touch the house. In parts, the adobe was breaking up, the porch steps were strewn with blowdown, the snake-fencing around the small yard was collapsed. Two cowboys had appeared on the staging around the house, but there was no other sign of activity.

Billy spoke very quietly. 'Where do you reckon the others are?'

'There's one way to find out, Billy. They're there; I can smell 'em.'

'I'd rather I could see 'em. What you plannin', Jed?'

'I ain't come this far to ride on, without seein' the old man.'

'You're not goin' to ride up to the front door?'

'Not without an advantage, I'm not.'

The two men sat quiet and alert on their horses. Jed was watching the scrub to the north. After ten minutes, he whistled short and sharp to get Billy's attention. He pointed to his left. 'Out beyond the corral. It's them again.'

It was the goup they'd seen earlier, riding into the thick mesquite. They'd now regrouped, headed for the broken fencing that partly screened the front of the ranch house. They appeared to be united and determined.

'I can see who they are now,' Billy said. 'It's Sebastian Pinto with his boys.'

Jed recalled the Pintos. For years they'd run cattle with the Cranes and neighbouring ranchers. They'd always been a kind and worthy family, and Jed wondered about the approaching confrontation on Indian Stone land.

He watched them cross the open ground, loose-reined with rifles cradled in their arms. Sebastian led them in. He sat easy and proud, on a fine criollo stallion.

Jed whispered gravely, 'There's something goin' on here we don't know about. I wonder if the Pintos do?' He turned to Billy, nodded back towards the brush. 'Let's move back a-ways.'

They backtracked, then circled until they neared the corral. Jed had a close look at the barn and bunkhouse. Both looked empty, but he didn't think they were. Like all the other ranch buildings they were thick-walled, baked solid, well fortified. He turned his attention back to the two men at the house.

He recognized one of them. A wild-looking man with a great, fat beard. He had the set of middle age, and wore filthy blue dungarees. He sat heavily in a chair and hawked a stream of tobacco juice between his boots.

'Chum Weems,' Jed murmured, and eked out a thin smile.

'Yeah, that's him,' Billy agreed. 'When we was kids, we reckoned you could smell him upwind. The other

93

one's a river rat from Waco. His name's Grit Bowler, and you wouldn't want to take him home with you.'

Jed was making a mental note of all he saw. After a full minute, his mind made up, he turned to Billy. 'That's a Henry repeater you've got there, Billy. Mind if I borrow it awhile?'

Billy pulled the rifle from its scabbard, and swung the stock towards Jed. He looked concerned as Jed levered a shell into the chamber. 'You aim to take 'em both from here?'

Jed, smiled back at him. 'No. I'm for heading off the Pintos. They could be the advantage we need.'

Jed turned his horse back towards the brush, but he was too late.

Weems and Bowler had moved back inside the house. A moment later, the criollo stepped elegantly from behind the snake-fencing into the front yard of the house.

* * *

After a slow advance of twenty yards, Sebastian Pinto checked his horse.

He turned to his oldest son. 'This is far enough, Olmedo. Take your brothers back into the brush. You know it's for me to do this alone. You will give me cover if it's needed.'

Olmedo's face burned with indignation. 'This is not for you to do alone. We are together. It's better that way. They will kill you, but for us.'

Sebastian stopped his son with the penetrating look of an elder. 'My mind is made up. You do as I say, Olmedo. Go now.'

Olmedo felt the cramp of frustration, but he glared at his brothers and obediently dug his heels into his horse.

The criollo threw its head into the air and snickered with insecurity. Sebastian held his rifle in one hand, keeping a light, close rein with the other. His eyes tunnelled straight ahead, looking for any sign of ambush.

He drew the horse in, swung the rifle back to the crook of his arm and faced the ranch house door. 'Gideon. Gideon Crane,' he called.

There was no response, and Sebastian glanced around him. He sensed danger, as a dog senses fear. From inside the house, a bolt was thrown, and he pointed the rifle towards the door.

A figure moved into the doorway. Gideon Crane hunched in a wheeled chair, clutching a stick. His eyes were staring level and hostile at Sebastian. 'What do you want with me? Get off my land.'

With equally bitter feeling, Sebastian addressed the aged rancher. 'Tell me about the men who killed my son, then I'll get off your land.'

Gideon Crane was instantly, visibly, shocked. 'I know nothing of a killing. Your son?'

'Manolito, my youngest one.' Sebastian tried hard to keep the authority. 'We found him yesterday. He was lying face down in the arroyo with a bullet in his chest. The water is still running red across your land, Gideon. The men that murdered him ride from here.'

Gideon dropped his stick, and his pale fingers clawed at the arms of his chair. His grizzled jaw trembled. 'Whatever's happening here, it don't involve killing children. You have my word on that, Sebastian. Little Mano, you say. I'm so sorry, I don't . . . '

Sebastian saw the breakdown of Gideon Crane's hostility, and he cut short the old man's anguish. 'And I'm sorry for what happened to you, Gideon, But it is to little effect now. You are responsible.'

Gideon's voice was hardly audible. 'You're sure they were from here?'

'I'm sure,' Sebastian said, levelly. 'They were pushing cattle, a lot of them mine. Manolito ran into them, and they shot him down. My son, Carlos, found his body. Together we trailed them to one of your corrals. It wasn't hard. We saw them working on the branding, from my Cactus Rose to Indian Stone.'

Sebastian turned his head slightly.

'You know nothing of that, also?'

Before there was any further response, a noisy dispute broke from inside the house. Gideon Crane turned his chair away from the doorway, and Sebastian sharply pulled back the criollo.

Both men heard someone cursing loudly. Then another voice cut the air. 'I can shoot you where you stand, Weems.'

10

Clearing the Land

There was a pause, a deep, rumbling cough, a sneer. Then a booming gunshot punched across the room behind the front door.

Within the instant crush of dead sound that followed, the girl's voice again rang clear. 'You cowardly scum. I'll kill you. He's riding away from here, now. Get out there and tell them.'

Chum Weems and Grit Bowler moved back on to the stoop. The girl followed closely, her face ashen, her eyes dark and flaming. She was pointing a .38 Yellowboy, which Jed immediately recognized.

He was in the mesquite, watching. He gritted his teeth, as the girl shoved the gleaming barrel at Weems. 'Do it,' she yelled at him. 'Tell them, he's to ride away. I'll send you to Hell now, if you don't.'

Weems raised his voice in alarm. 'Get the Mex outa here, boys. She means it.'

Cowboys shambled from the bunk-house into the yard. Some were sniggering, but they were all fascinated by the sight of Chummy Weems stuck on the end of Lena's carbine. Rough, jingo Texans had their own ideas about a woman's place.

One of them called out, but, because of the situation, it lacked conviction. 'An' if we don't, you cain't be shootin' us all, ma'am.'

Lena tossed her hair and sniffed. 'I don't aim to, *mister*. This stinking old bag'll get it first, then it'll be your turn. Now go ahead. Make up your mind.'

The Weems method of staying alive, was to know when to back off. It was he who 'fought and ran away'. With a ring of steel hard between his shoulder blades, he spat drily. 'It's the jailbreaker we want, boys, an' I got a feelin' she'll use this popgun. You let Pinto ride in safe enough, now we can all watch him ride out the same way,' he added with bite.

Just behind Weems, Grit Bowler said, 'We can take care o' him some other time.' The man from Waco smirked, and took a step towards Lena.

Weems glowered at Sebastian Pinto. 'You heard, chilligut. Clear out.'

Sebastian removed his sombrero, and ran his fingers through silver-stubbled hair. His eyes blistered Weems, then settled on the girl. 'My thanks, *señora*. Come and visit an old Mex, sometime.' He nodded courteously.

As he cantered out of the yard, Weems called after him, 'We'll all come and visit.'

All eyes followed Sebastian, and Lena relaxed a little. She allowed the barrel of the carbine to drop, and Bowler seized the opportunity. He lashed out, gripped the gun, and wrenched it from Lena's hands. 'Now then, you pretty little bitch,' he breathed into her face, 'let's hear what you've got to say about this.'

But the threat was hardly uttered, before Weems jumped him. Slamming his elbow into Bowler's ribs, Weems shouted, 'Gimme the gun.' With an ugly oath, he swept the barrel into line with Sebastian Pinto's retreating back.

★　★　★

For all his furious haste, Weems wasn't fast enough to make the shot. The noise of a Henry repeating rifle crashed out across the yard, and behind Weems a window exploded into a thousand fragments. There was no time for anyone on the stoop to move, before Jed's voice followed up. 'Drop the gun, Weems. Throw it into the yard.'

As shattered as the window, Weems gasped. He didn't understand quickly enough, and stared straight ahead. Then his eyes jumped around, looking for the gunman in the brush. He tossed the carbine out in front of him, and Jed called again, 'Don't get foolhardy. I can kill any one of you from here.'

'Who the hell's that?' Weems glared swiftly at Bowler, who'd been considering a move.

Weems was breathing heavily, shaking with confusion, but he retained the survival instinct.

'I'm Jed Crane,' Jed shouted. 'Rule's jailbreaker. The man you've been waiting for.' A spiky silence followed, before Jed spoke again. 'You two men, take a good look at the window behind you; then unbuckle your gunbelts.'

Jed tracked the rifle between Weems and Bowler. If one of them was going to break the stand-off, he wasn't sure who it would be. They were pushed and unpredictable. He remained tense, his finger gently feeling the trigger.

Weems said something to Bowler, and they removed their guns. Weems swung his belt out alongside him, and Bowler let his drop around his feet.

Jed whistled low through his teeth. He'd have preferred a better time for getting involved, but Weems's attempt at backshooting Sebastian Pinto, gave him no choice.

He started at a snap and crackle behind him, turned his head fractionally, as a horse nosed forward. Billy Newton appeared, shifting through the tangled mesquite.

'I got to the Pintos,' Billy said uneasily. 'They're all ready, if you need 'em.'

'Let's find out,' Jed said. Without taking his eyes off Weems and Bowler, he yelled towards the ranch house. 'You're all trespassing on Crane land. Get off it now, before I decide to kill somebody.'

As Jed rose, and stepped forward, the yard was suddenly bordered with horsemen. It was Sebastian Pinto and his boys, bristling with weapons. Billy crabbed his horse close alongside Jed.

Chum Weems took a step forward, wiping a stained hand across his mouth. 'Jed Crane. I shoulda guessed,' he said, resignedly. 'Come back for a wash and brush up, eh?'

'Yeah, well it's somethin' you'd never know about, Weems,' Jed answered roughly. 'You'll always smell like the end of a buffalo. An' talkin' of that, when you see your boy, Lipper, you can tell him I'm coming for him. Him and Scranton.'

Weems dragged out a scornful threat. 'Lipper's no angel, Crane, but he's my son, and he's no killer. You'll have to go through me.'

Jed stared coldly across the yard, as he walked slowly forward. 'Your boy knows how a kid out huntin' rabbits gets slaughtered, and somebody's gonna pay for the death of my brother. Whether you get in the way's up to you.'

'You always were full a piss an' wind, Crane. But we ain't talkin' that stuff any more. You've fallen into a pit fulla vipers. As from now, you don't have more'n days to live.'

Jed stepped up tight to Weems. 'Well then, snake breath, I'll make the most of what time's left.'

Without taking his eyes from the

man's face, Jed swung the barrel of his rifle across Weems's shins. Weems yelled in pain and, as he went down to grab his legs, Jed slammed his bunched knuckles hard into the side of his head. 'I'm fast tirin' of your mouth, Weems. Now stay downwind, and get off this land.'

As Weems and Bowler slouched indolently towards the corral, Billy Newton looked up from collecting the gunbelts. 'Hey,' he called out. 'How you gettin' back to town?'

Both men stared back at him.

'Can't see any of your horses in the corral.' Billy looked at Jed, and smiled. 'There's only Indian Stone mounts in there.'

The implication, dawned on Bowler. 'It's twenty-five miles to Juno Flats.'

'I'd say closer to thirty. Without guns an' horses, you'll be mighty hard-pressed. I doubt if you'll make it fer breakfast,' Billy snapped.

As the men began their walk out into the brush, Sebastian Pinto watched from his criollo. He was curt, but as civil as he'd been to Lena.

He said, 'I am in your debt, friend. We will meet soon, there is maybe a future to discuss. Now, my sons and I have to drive that herd of animals off your land.'

A callous edge crept into his voice. 'I still need to know how Manolito died. Perhaps between here and the town, someone will tell me. Who knows?' Pinto touched his sombrero. '*Adios*.'

Jed watched them go. He turned to Billy. 'I don't know about the future, Billy, but something tells me he'll find out who shot his boy.'

11

The Crane Family

When Jed walked on to the stoop, his shoulders hunched, Rafelena was waiting. By the look in her eyes, it was obvious the shock had got to her.

'Ma'am,' he said, uncertain of the full name, or the use of Lena. 'I see you found my old Yellowboy.'

Her mouth was trembling, as she tried for a response. 'I know how to use a gun. Weems was going to shoot Mr Pinto through the window.'

'It would have been his head, more'n likely.' Jed smiled at his little joke. 'And if you'd really known how to shoot, you'd have taken it off.'

Lena smiled, and it broke the approach. 'So you're Jed?'

'Yeah, that's him,' a voice rattled,

from just inside the door. 'He don't visit much.'

Jed looked in at his father. He expected to see a physical change, but the old man in the wheeled chair was a long way off the Gideon Crane he remembered. In the haggard terrain of his father's face, only the long nose remained as a landmark.

'Dad?' he said, staring at the tortuous clasp of his father's hands.

The aged rancher sat, scowling 'Where the hell you been? It's been years.'

Jed's emotions were confused, and he went for a vague response. 'Most places . . . border points . . . looked over the edges.'

Gideon rubbed at his grizzled chin. 'Well, you don't look like you got rich in the lookin'. What yer doin' with them Pintos? You come back to take off me as well?'

'What have the Pintos taken from you, Dad? From what I hear, it sounds like it's Indian Stone that's been on the grab.'

'No. They're all stealin' from me.'

The old man was shaking with anger. 'Them Mexicans have been helpin' themselves. They're no better than . . . than . . . ' Gideon's attitude changed slightly. 'I know nothin' about the boy, Manolito. I swear it.'

'I believe that, Dad, but Rule knew about it. He knew about Milo too.' Jed gave his father a penetrating look. 'What's all this really about? It's more than cattle rustling. They've got something else. They're running the ranch as if it's theirs.'

Gideon banged his hands on his knees, but looked defiant. 'You come back here, after all these years, and without so much as a word. You start tellin' me what's so. There's ways of skinnin' a cat. Learn some,' he snapped.

Jed saw the torture within his old man, and knew he'd hit the raw nerve. He also felt a gnawing fear of the unknown. 'You can tell me about it,' he said tentatively. 'Your story, not what I'm surmisin'.'

The shadow of a near-forgotten smile crossed Gideon's face. He turned around, and looked over to where Rafelena was standing, tactfully quiet. 'Yeah, this is the youngest one, Lena. Jed.' He looked back up at Jed. 'Lena's been the daughter I never had. Don't know what I'd do without her, now.'

Jed eased his way into the room. 'Perhaps you won't have to,' he muttered.

Lena glanced at the men's faces, and blinked a few times. 'I know,' she said. 'We're all starved.'

Gideon turned on Billy Newton, and his eyes narrowed. 'You ain't been invited.'

Jed's chin sank to his chest, and he swore, exasperated. He glared at his father. 'It was Billy who got me outa jail. You'd want me swingin' from a tree somewhere? Christ, there's some rotten peel around you.'

Billy was already backing away towards the stoop.

Jed stepped towards him. 'I know

how you feel,' he said. 'Perhaps I should never have come back. Let's go.'

As they made towards the yard, Gideon ran his chair against the door post. 'Goddamn it, you only just arrived,' he yelled.

Billy turned. 'I've never done anything to harm you or yours, Mr Crane, and you know it.' He looked sadly at Jed, and carried on towards his horse.

Jed turned back to Gideon. 'Yeah, Milo and Billy took some beef. Beef that had already been stolen from the ranchers round here. They sold it back to 'em, for a dollar a head.'

'They sold 'em back?' Gideon queried.

'That's right, Mr Crane, you included,' Billy joined in. 'Ranch owners got some cattle back, and me an' Milo made a few dollars. We was kids, an' we earned it.'

'Buck Rule knew about this, did he? He found out?'

'Yeah,' Billy said. 'He found out. That's the real reason Milo was shot. If

I'd been with him, they'd have got me too.'

Gideon looked at both men, and for many moments, no one said a word. Then he wrinkled his nose and pushed himself back inside the house. 'That's as maybe,' they heard him say. 'Can't help it if I heard different.'

Jed shrugged his shoulders, raised his eyebrows at Billy. 'Well, now the apologies are done an' dusted, let's see if that food's anywhere near ready. I'm getting real tired of stock-feed.'

★   ★   ★

They moved into the main room of the house, and the nostalgia immediately crowded in on Jed.

There was the French piano, a Victorian writing desk, a dresser filled with blue-patterned china, a big, scrubbed-pine table and a dozen and one other small reminders of a better past. All of it freighted to this remote Texas wilderness by his father. Most of it had been to please Jed's mother, in a land so harsh and different from her southern upbringing.

He looked at the big mantel over the stone fireplace. He'd never forgotten the stern pictures that had watched him all these years. One, huge and oval-framed of his grandfather, the other smaller, and even more severe of his father. But it all brought back the carefree, spirited memories of his childhood.

During the meal, conversation was still strained, but a little easier than it had been. After they'd eaten, Jed sat on the stoop with his father. Billy, tactfully, stayed inside.

'Tell me about you breaking out of jail.'

'How I got in there's more interesting,' Jed answered. 'They would have killed me. It wasn't the first time. Billy turned the tables on 'em.'

'How'd you get tangled with Rule in the first place?'

'I didn't. It wasn't him in the first

place.' Jed told his story, while his father sat, engrossed, but uncomfortable. He told of the confrontation in Chimney Point, and the attempt on his life after being trailed. 'That's where Rule turned up, spoke of me being a Crane, or not.'

Jed looked keenly at his father. 'You know what he meant by that, don't you, Dad?'

'I know what he meant,' Gideon growled. 'You've probably guessed most of it. He's set to take over the ranch, an' there's not much I can do about it. I'm financially ruined.' Gideon looked hollow-eyed at Jed. 'But there's somethin' else.'

Jed detected helpless suffering, as his father carried on. 'There's something he's stringing me out with.' He paused, adjusting to his misery. 'It's about your mother, and Lena. Rule claims to have something on her.'

'What? On who?' Jed was amazed.

'Lena. But it goes back to your mother. He reckons, Lena's *her* daughter. It would have happened in Atlanta.'

'You believe all this? You had no idea?'

'No. How could I? No reason to suspect. I never knew her then, of course. I couldn't have known.'

'What proof's Rule got? Has he told you that?'

'That's what he knows . . . what he says.'

'Lena's my sister?'

'Half-sister. Yes.'

'Does she know?'

'She don't know a thing. Anyone that knows the truth will be dead an' buried by now. That's why he gets his own way. Can you get a handle on that?'

'Yeah, I think so. Has he threatened to tell her?'

'No.'

'Did it hurt bad, when you found out?'

'Not by the time I began to believe it. There was always a streak there, the way she looks, sometimes.'

Jed looked back into the house, but

didn't think they were being overheard. 'I can see what you meant by the 'daughter you never had'.' He suddenly looked at his father suspiciously. 'You don't think there's anything between 'em, do you?'

Who? Lena and Rule? Hell, no. But it may be something *he's* got his mind on.'

'You must have thought of shooting him, Dad?'

'Every time I see him.'

Gideon and Jed sat quiet, both with their own thoughts. Jed knew how ordinary folk responded to hearsay. They weren't as big on tolerance as they were on bigotry in that part of the West. Lena would carry stigma, and it would reflect back on Gideon. It would be simple enough in the telling, but the result would be cruel and lasting.

Gideon went on to tell what he knew of the past, but Jed wasn't listening. He was trying to get his mind set on what to do.

Gideon poked a bony finger into

Jed's leg. His voice had recovered a touch of its former grittiness. 'Like I said. She's been here while you were gone. There was no one else.'

'Yeah, I understand,' Jed spoke quietly. 'There's no argument with that.'

There was another silence, then Gideon said, 'What's to do, Son? Seems like we're in a hell of a mess. Your prospects ain't much if you stay here.'

Jed touched his father's shoulder. 'Whatever it takes, Dad. You ain't the only one with trouble on his back. I'll be leavin' shortly. I'll take Billy.'

'Where you goin'?'

'Rule's packing a herd up to Chimney Point. That's where we'll make a start.' Briefly, Jed explained what was on his mind, and Gideon listened, growing tired and bemused.

'With help, you might get away with it.' Gideon, nodded thoughtfully to himself. 'I'll get you a note on ownership. You'll need it.'

Gideon turned and wheeled himself

back into the house. It had been dark a long time, and Jed sat with his back against the cool, adobe wall and fretted. He sensed a movement close behind him, and turned his head. Lena was looking up at the moon that gleamed, wafer thin.

He couldn't think of anything to say. He thought of some of the mush that Billy had been delivering earlier, then realized he was staring at her. 'Hi. Come to have a look at the night?' he said. The situation made it difficult for him, and Lena didn't know why.

She said, 'I was going to say, you look worried, but decided not to. It would have been pretty dumb. For what it's worth, Jed, I'm glad you came back. I don't suppose you can tell, but your pa already looks better. Some of his spirit's returned.'

'I never knew about the accident with his legs.'

'That's when he got worse. When he became suspicious of his friends.

Sometimes, I think he includes me in his darkness.' Lena's voice began to break with emotion. 'You will help, won't you? He won't come out and say it, but he needs you. We both do. There's no one else to turn to.'

Gideon rolled out on to the stoop between them. With a curious look of concern, he broke into their talk. 'Smelled burnin' from somewhere near, turned out to be my own ears.' He sounded sarcastic, but it wasn't aggressive or provocative.

Lena went back into the house, and Gideon held up a piece of paper for Jed. 'Here's your authority on the herd and the ranch. Keep it safe. I'm off to bed now. Goodnight, Son.' That was all he had to say. He shivered from the cool night breeze that blew across the range, and went back inside.

Alone in the darkness, Jed shoved the written document into his coat and forgot it. He was still thinking of Lena, and his mother, but there was another problem.

When it was known where he'd been, and what he'd done in the years since Galesburg, he'd rank alongside Lena. His father was wrong about being in a hell of a mess. It was far worse.

12

Round-Up

Jed Crane and Billy Newton left the house well before sun-up. The land still held its night chill, and the day's first breezes cut through the mesquite. They rode side by side. Sometimes the horses closed up, other times the dense brush wedged their trails apart. The men were wrapped in silence, each with their own thoughts, but then dawn yielded the clamour of aroused bird and desert critter.

Jed had his doubts about leaving Indian Stone undefended. It worried him, but he didn't believe Rule would actually order retribution, or that Gideon or Lena were in immediate danger. Rule knew what he wanted, but it didn't mean he'd run himself ragged for the sake of a few days. It was different for him and Billy, though. By now, they could be printed-up members of a gang of outlaws; prey to anyone who carried a gun.

Billy was taking Jed to see a friend. A modest cattle rancher, and a breaker of mustangs for army forts along the Rio Grande.

As grey light fused into blue, they skirted tangles of chaparral, now lively with jack-rabbit and junco finches. The small ranch and its out-buildings were hugger-mugger in the bend of a creek.

Billy Newton greeted the man who'd seen their traildust from a long way off. He was introduced as Eben Tubbs, a slim, muscular man, dressed in worn denim and leather chaps.

Jed and Billy sat drinking coffee on the low step outside Eben's log cabin. Eben sat on a stump, telling of how, and more than once, he'd surprised someone driving off a few of his precious longhorns or a saddlebroke mustang. Not much in Texas terms, but to Eben, the difference between sink or swim.

'They were Rule's men?' asked Jed.

'Can't be certain, but who else could they be?' Tubbs said. 'Only Rule could put together a big enough made-up herd. He could provide the protection you'd need.'

'Got any plans?' Jed asked.

'Not really, no. What plannin' can you do, when you're so much out on your own?'

Jed nodded understandingly, and thought for a moment. 'Don't stay out on your own. Join me an' Billy. What have you got to lose?'

'You've somethin' in mind?'

'Yeah, I'm gonna hit Rule. When the time's right, I could use some help. With you, we'll be up to three.'

Eben made a wry smile. 'You just asked what I'd got to lose: with those odds, it'd probably be my life.'

Billy spoke up. 'We'll get more. There must be more ranchers who've lost stock to Rule's men. There's the Pintos to begin with. They've lost many a head. I reckon the old man gritted his teeth for the sake of a quiet life. But they made a mistake in killing little Manolito. Sebastian an' his boys won't ever let that rest.'

'Yeah. You've got yourself another gun if you want it.' Eben declared his hand. 'How you fixin' to hit him?' he went on. 'I can get some help. Tom Needle'll join us. He's just lost a string a yearlings.'

Jed stood up. 'Rule's organizin' a drive up to Chimney Point. From what I've seen an' heard, Rule calls the tune in most of Langtry County. He rubs with the army and the damn carpetbaggers. But he's still got to drive that herd to Chimney Point. There's no law to speak of west of the plateau. Even the Rangers give it room.'

Billy jumped to his feet alongside Jed. 'That's it. We hit him out on the plateau. We'll pay him back some.'

'It won't be a junket, Billy. Those men of his are hard. They're mean, an' they don't bother much about observing custom. You know; whether you're in the right or not.'

The men looked at each other enthusiastically.

Jed said to Eben, 'After we've called up your man Needle, we'll ride to the Pinto ranch.'

'Good,' Eben replied. Then he nodded to his cabin. 'Come on, I'll cook us up some breakfast, before we go. I've a clutch of fresh hen eggs.'

* * *

The men dismounted on a slanting bluff. They stood, holding in their horses, looking north. From miles away, a shadow of dust billowed low; the herd spilled like tan crumbs on the burnished range.

'Early tomorrow will be a good time,' suggested Sebastian Pinto, his gaze fixed on the cloud ahead. 'Tomorrow, or maybe — '

'No maybes,' Jed Crane said quickly.

'We're running out o' time. We'll hit 'em while they're still off the border.'

He watched the slow-moving herd. For days they'd followed, keeping well out of sight, walking the straps of the Edwards Plateau, from West Texas to within thirty miles of the Oklahoma border.

Jed knew they had to make their move before the herd crossed the border. An attack in Oklahoma could easily run them up against soldiers out of a Cimarron River fort.

That far, they'd let Buckminster Rule's trail crew drift the cattle north, but it would only be *that* far. Once again, he considered their chances. The Rule outfit was made up of ten riders. Jed was going up against them with Billy Newton, Eben Tubbs, Tom Needle, Sebastian Pinto and his three boys. They were down in numbers, but courage and surprise might even it up a bit, he thought. If it didn't, it was the wind up for him, and everyone else.

'We'll make our last camp below the next ridge,' he said. 'Cold harbour, not even coffee. I want everyone ready early. We'll take them just before sun-up.'

'Where will you be, then?' asked Billy.

'The cattle will be bedded down soon. I'm gonna take a wide swing east, then north. Have a closer look at the land. I'll be back sometime after dark.'

★ ★ ★

Jed rode east. He kept hidden, making gain from every rib of land around the plateau. He used his eyes well, seeking firmer ground, close in to windblown rises, and tangles of brush. It was the Indian way of tracking, and Jed understood it.

He found where the herd would be settled for the night. The chuckwagon was ahead, unhitched, and pointing north, bankside to a fork of the North Canadian River. Jed sat and quartered the land. The arroyo was edged with shrubby birch and willow. Bunchgrass spread out in thick clumps from the rested chuckwagon.

Jed loose-hobbled his horse, and through the grass he crawled to within fifty feet of the wagon. The cook was limping around the new fire, laying a skillet and pulling cans from the store box. He was making ready for camp supper, and Jed watched him shaping curses that went with the task. They'd all have something to complain about early next morning, he was thinking.

He looked out at the herd coming in. The point riders were already turning the lead steers into their milling rest. He'd seen enough then, and he crawled along the arroyo bank a-ways, even managed to pull up a root for the gelding.

Time was moving on, shadows were merging into the flat greyness of evening. To the east, where Billy Newton should be setting out a cold-harbour camp, the scrub-covered ridge was just touching the sun as it settled into the range.

13

Hand to Hand

Jed had ridden back three or four miles when he heard the unmistakable sound of gunfire fracture the range. He pulled in his horse to listen, and heard two more gunshots, before silence closed in again. His heartbeat quickened, as he realized the firing came from the direction of their camp, near the still distant ridge. With a sinking, gut feeling he shouted, and raced his horse.

Running at speed, fusing with his horse, using cast of the land for cover was something Jed knew about. He'd learned the hard way, where grisly torture or death waited for mistakes. The Comanche were good for the learning, if you lived long enough to profit by it.

For nearly a mile, he tore along the

bed of the arroyo, before swinging his horse out on to the low bank. There was a clearing ahead of him with no brush cover, but without slowing, he drove hard across it. The horse's hooves pounded the soil, the only sound Jed noticed, until it joined the thudding discord of fast closing riders.

He had the time to swing around, but only back into the shallow cover of the arroyo. He had to go forward, to try and make the slope with its scrub cover. Camp should be somewhere in the lee of the ridge, less than a quarter mile. A few more minutes was all he needed.

He never made the cover. In the closing darkness, the riders came at him. There were two of them, but Jed couldn't make out any features. They were on to him too suddenly, and from astride a pale horse, one of them had already levelled his gun. It exploded within twenty paces of Jed, as he pulled his Walker Colt.

With the report of the gunshot crashing around his head, Jed didn't slow. He rode on, until at point-blank range, he shot into the body of the man who'd fired. There was a tormented whinny, then he cannoned on, into the second rider. The mare shuddered and reeled from the impact of muscle, but Jed regained control, as the other horse and rider fell to the ground. He swerved away, but from close distance, turned and sat for a moment while his own horse took in great lungsful of air. He watched, as the man who'd been thrown, scrambled clear of his saddle and stirrups. Jed actioned his Colt again, as the shaken rider looked for the rifle he'd been carrying.

The fallen horse lurched back to its feet, its eyes bulging with fright, and its body trembling. The rider looked around nervously, then walked slowly to where his partner was lying dead.

Jed edged his horse up behind the man. 'Don't make any more dumb moves, mister, unless you want to join him,' Jed snapped.

The man got to his feet slowly, and

gaped up at Jed. Again, he glanced at the ground around him. 'I ain't got nothin' to make a dumb move with,' he answered, dispiritedly.

Jed grunted. 'Tell me who you are, an' what you're doing here.'

'I'm not certain.' The man turned away from Jed. He was trying to get himself together, trying to figure out a credible line. 'We were out lookin' to make camp. You know the rest.'

Jed almost laughed. 'Yeah, and I was out takin' the evenin' air.' He nodded at the man on the ground. 'He dead?'

'From that close, he was dead before he hit the ground,' was the sour response.

'That's a hell of a price to pay for a campsite,' Jed muttered. 'Now, I've already asked you once, what're you doin' out here?'

The man took a long, deep-rasping breath. 'Scoutin' for Indian Stone. We're on the drive to Chimney Point.'

Jed got a short stab of pain behind his temple and swallowed hard. 'What was the gunfire, back along the ridge?'

'We been keepin' watch on riders that've been doggin' the herd. Been south of us for days. We caught up with 'em. Shot their camp up a bit.'

Jed's heart was thumping with anguish. 'Sounded to me like they made a fight back.'

The man was unnerved by Jed's scrutiny. 'Pekker figured he hit one or two, but weren't sure. There was more of 'em than we thought. I'm paid for scoutin', not gunfightin'.'

Jed wanted to know more. 'What made you think they were after the herd?'

'Indian Stone sent out a rider to warn us, Mr Rule said to look out for riders that came too close. Fellow called Crane, would probably be at the head of 'em.'

The man stopped suddenly, and looked curiously at Jed. 'Say, who the hell are you, mister?'

'Jed. Jed Crane. And that'll be my father who owns Indian Stone, not Mr

Rule, as you so quaintly seem to think.'

Jed dismounted and walked straight to the man. 'Now there's one or two things to clear up, scouting man.' He kicked out at the scout's kneecaps and watched coldly as the man sank painfully to his knees.

Jed took a step back. 'I've told you who I am; now who the hell are *you*, scout, and who's in charge out there?'

The man was back on his feet. He held out his hands submissively, in a slow, and awkward movement. 'They call me Ivy. I'm a scout for the drive. That's all I was hired for,' he said, but it was only a deception for what the man had in mind.

The open palm of his right hand suddenly clenched tight, and he swung his fist upwards, aiming for the front of Jed's face.

But Jed had sensed the movement, and before it plugged-in, he sidestepped as Ivy stumbled forward. He was temporarily off balance, and Jed ripped a quick blow up and into his head. It was vicious, and cracked Ivy's nose, immediately spurting flecks of dark blood across his face.

Ivy snorted and his legs buckled, as he gurgled air into his throat. His eyes were eager and glaring, and Jed quickly hit him again. It was like striking pebbles and he could feel wet mush on his fingers as pain lacerated his arm and right shoulder. Ivy was furious and stamped forward, ignoring the blows. He was rough and strong, even smirking as he came on. He flung his arms wide to draw Jed into him. Jed flat-footed two, then three steps backwards. He waited until Ivy rushed, then with both fists, swung hard. He almost lost his footing, and it wasn't enough to put Ivy down.

Ivy squeezed his eyes, then bluffed left to swing a hard loop with his right arm. Jed was surprised, and took a lot of the pain on his forearm, but the fist smashed sharp and severe into his ribs. He blinked several times as the shock wave pulsed across his chest. It was momentary, but in the distraction another blow smacked into his forehead. It sent him toppling down, hard and flat, on his shoulder blades. He drew his knees in close, and rolled sideways as Ivy came leaping in. He was cursing and stomping with a boot heel, hoping to thrust the rasping wedge somewhere into Jed's face. The kick grated across Jed's scalp and, as he pushed himself to his feet, Ivy moved towards him.

The scout came in again, and Jed stood his ground, watching the reckless bending swing of the man's fist. It was easy to dodge, and Jed stepped inside, making a hard stab into the knotted flesh of Ivy's neck.

Ivy gasped for breath, and threw out his arms wildly. He locked his fingers around Jed's back, clutching them tight against his spine. The pressure got worse as Ivy crushed the peppery sweat of his body into Jed's face.

Jed felt himself being lifted off his feet, and he struggled to keep his heels on the ground. His arms and legs were losing their control and, as his breath turned shallow, he twisted his head away from the vile closeness of the scout.

As Jed wearied himself into submission, Ivy mistook the effect of his grip and relaxed his hold slightly, long enough for Jed to respond and wrench his arms free. Without pausing he threw his hands under Ivy's jaw and jerked upwards. Ivy immediately tried to tighten his arms, but Jed had the advantage. He straightened his hand and snapped his knuckles into the point of Ivy's Adam's apple. The man instantly fell away, fractured with soundless agony as he clutched at his throat.

Ivy was making odd retching noises as he shambled around Jed. He spread his arms and they weaved slowly, cobra-like, trying to catch Jed's eye. He got closer and closer, then kicked out, his foot catching Jed in the right knee. The blow sent Jed sprawling, and he spreadeagled, landing with his face shoved into the hard, trampled ground.

Jed twisted on to his back, and kicked out with his feet. The dipping sun caught his eyes, and Ivy's figure became vague and blurred. But the blow connected, his heels driving hard into the bone of kneecaps. The impact felled Ivy like a woodsman's axe, and he fell with an arm stretched across Jed's waist. Before he could recover, Jed bounded to his feet and smashed his bunched fist down at the arch of Ivy's neck. Then he drove short chopping blows into the man's sinewy shoulders.

Ivy tried to draw his knees up, but failed, and collapsed as another blow took him full and low in the back. He rolled from side to side, trying to extricate himself, spitting blood from his smashed mouth as Jed stood over him. He managed to unwind into a crouch, his face and hair smeared with sweat and masked with dirt. He swayed and trod himself into a tight circle while Jed took a step backwards.

'Now, I'll ask you again: who's running that herd?' Jed rasped.

Ivy spat into the ground. 'George McCluskey. They're all Rule's men. Me an' Pekker were the only ones that weren't. I've already told you.'

'One other thing.' Jed winced at his bruised ribs. 'This word you had from Juno Flats? Was there mention of back-up for McCluskey?'

The scout looked as though he'd had enough talk, but as Jed took a painful impatient breath, he spluttered back a response. 'They're sending a posse out. Lepe Scranton's ridin' with it.'

'Scranton,' Jed repeated, slowly.

'Yeah, You've met him, have you?' The spite was plain in Ivy's voice.

'We've met,' said Jed. The anger burst from him as he turned away from the scout. 'Get back to the herd,' he yelled. 'When you get there, tell McCluskey to expect a visit real soon. Tell him Jed Crane's coming to take his herd back.'

Jed rode away to the ridge. He kicked his heels deep, his insides knotted with the dread of what he'd find.

14

Death at the Camp

There was nobody in sight when Jed rode close to the camp. It was full dark, as he twisted silently through the clumps of brush. He stared into the darkness, but couldn't see much, save the black silhouettes of cottonwood.

He eased his Colt from his waistband, gave a short, sharp whistle, and waited for a response. After a minute or two, a sound, then a movement, caught his attention, and he made a cautious, muffled call. 'Over here.'

A rider stepped his horse forward, and spoke quietly. 'That you, Jed? We been expectin' you.'

It was Billy Newton, and Jed eased forward to meet him. 'What happened, Billy?'

'They rode in on us, less than an

hour ago. Just started shooting. Felipe took most of it. Eben got hit.'

'How bad?'

'Eben'll live, but Felipe's real bad.'

Jed didn't say anything except, 'Show me where.'

Billy swung his horse around, and Jed followed. He was wondering what to say, thinking of his blunder in leaving the men alone. He hadn't considered that George McCluskey would have a scout; that they'd been watched, ever since leaving Langtry County. While he'd gone to poke his nose around the range, they'd taken the time to shoot up his own men. He swore savagely, and looked to the stars.

Billy stopped and turned his head. 'What's up?' he called back.

Jed rode alongside. 'Sorry, I was just thinkin' about it. Tell me how it happened.'

'Young Felipe was supposed to be on watch. Wasn't his fault though. Wouldn't have been much trouble to gun him down. They knew what they were doin'; he didn't, poor kid.'

Jed made a sharp, guttural sound in his throat, and Billy carried on explaining.

'He managed to shoot back, though. None of us knew what was goin' on. We were firing into the night; just lying on the ground shootin'; couldn't see clearly, except the powder flashes.'

'What happened then?'

'They musta rode off.' Billy could see Jed's face, pale in the darkness. 'We heard a couple gunshots sometime after. Was that you, Jed?'

Jed was already thinking on how he'd let the second man off with his life; how he'd sent him back with the message to McCluskey. But he hadn't known for sure then what had happened. He told Billy the story of the run-in and his fight.

Billy looked hard again at Jed's face. 'Yeah I thought there was somethin' wrong, I can see now. You all right?'

Jed avoided the question. 'Scranton's after us with a posse.'

'You want we should call it off?'

It was about the only thing that made sense to Jed. They'd lost another rider, and McCluskey would soon be joined by Scranton and his men. Jed's intent was shaping up for a rout. He was holding the broken straight.

'I can't ask any of you to do any more, Billy. I'll finish it alone if I have to.'

'No need. Sebastian's in no frame o' mind to ride away. He's lost two of his boys, it looks like. The others'll stay. We've already decided, Jed. We'll stay for as long as it takes.'

Night breezes scuffled the brush as they rode the lee of the ridge. The creak of tack, and snorting from the horses were the only sounds that broke the silence. After a few hundred yards Billy pulled up and called into the darkness. A voice replied, and they dismounted.

A small fire burned in the blowdown and colourless scrub. In the margins of firelight, figures were just visible, some lying, and others kneeling. Beyond, the horses made uneasy sounds against their hobbles.

Billy and Jed walked towards the fire, where Sebastian Pinto was crouched beside a body. He looked up, but didn't speak. Jed kneeled down to look at the body that was rolled into a blanket. 'Oh no,' he groaned, and stared tragically at Sebastian. He took off his Stetson, and ran a hand over his bruised face. 'I'm sorry, Sebastian. I didn't know he was dead.'

Sebastian spoke without looking up. 'He was fourteen years old.'

Jed didn't know on whom to vent his frustration and anger. He'd told them, a cold camp. That meant *no fire*. It could have been their mistake. He didn't say anything; it just evened up the blunders.

After a few uneasy moments, Sebastian looked to Jed. He was shaken, drained of emotion. 'Two of my boys,' he said. 'Fine boys. When do we go for those responsible?'

There was another difficult silence.

Then Billy stepped up between the two men. 'We know they're one less, Sebastian. Jed shot one of their riders, less than two hours ago.'

Sebastian grunted and gave Jed a 'was it worth it?', look.

Jed moved away to see Eben Tubbs, who was sitting with his back to a stunted yucca. Beside him, sat Olmedo and Carlos, both staring towards the guttering fire. He mumbled some words of understanding, but they didn't respond. Jed accepted that; they'd just lost another brother.

Eben had a leg wound. He'd cut through his chaps, and Jed saw a neck cloth, bound tight. 'It's no more'n a scuff,' he said, when Jed asked him about it. 'Ain't gonna slow me up none.' Then he asked, 'What do we do now?'

Jed knew it was time for him to make a decision, and he spoke fast and clear. 'Now we know what we're really up against. The odds of us coming out of it all in one piece, ain't gonna get any better. There's not a lot of time, and if we're gonna move, it'll have to be fast. What do you say?'

'I've told you,' Billy said. 'Whatever it takes. We're together.'

Jed nodded. 'I told you, the odds ain't improved. Lepe Scranton's riding from Juno Flats. He's comin' with a posse. If they meet up with McCluskey that'll more than likely double their numbers, and they'll be ready for us. But if we go for Scranton now, maybe we stand a chance.'

'Difficult to surprise 'em in this land,' Tom Needle said. 'If that's what you mean?'

'There's ways of using the land. But we have to move now.'

'What about the herd?' asked Eben. 'They'll have moved right up to the border, maybe even crossed it.'

'If we wait until Scranton joins up, you're right, but it'll take the herd at least a whole day to make Oklahoma, maybe a bit longer. If we go for Scranton early enough, we can still catch 'em.'

Sebastian raised himself from beside the body of Felipe. He looked keenly at Jed. 'Then we move,' he said firmly. 'But first, with your help, I will bury my son.'

★ ★ ★

Before early light spilled from the east, they were nearly thirty miles south. Jed hardly blinked as he stared across the plateau. He'd sat, unmoving, for hours, the Indian way. It was still cold, and Jed felt icy rivers of sweat running down his neck and across his shoulders. The silence, and scope of the open range was overpowering, and his heart thumped fast.

The night before, Sebastian and his boys had scraped a shallow grave for Felipe. To keep off coyotes, they'd shaped a mound of chaparral and small stones. Without mention, they'd all felt it wasn't much of a last resting place.

But Jed was now occupied with the present. He had to find Scranton, who was somewhere out on the plateau. He'd spot him all right, but there wasn't going to be a best time. The only certainty was that they were there, somewhere.

Another hour on, and a faint whiff drifted towards him, as a low desert breeze suddenly curled downwind. It was the thin reek of woodsmoke, but Jed didn't move. The Scranton camp was closer than he'd thought, and the reason for his stealthy patience.

He peered into the shadowless landscape, tracing a line of scrub along a dry creek. He spotted the camp as the first wisps of colour broke from the eastern horizon.

Low against the skyline, Jed made his way back to camp. The men gathered around him, anxious, and fixed on action.

'They're a mile off, camped alongside a creek. I couldn't make out a guard, but it won't be a free fight.' Jed looked at the tight faces around him. 'We'll hit them hard and fast; it's the only way.'

'We hit them with everything we have,' said Sebastian Pinto. 'We have the surprise.'

'That's right, Sebastian, but we have to ride away again.' Jed didn't need more death on his already heavy conscience. 'We'll all have a job to do when we come back for the herd, remember.' Jed turned to Eben Tubbs.

'Eben, you know horses. It'll be up to you and Tom to take care of 'em. Run 'em off when you hear the first shots.'

'Yeah, but they'll be tied in, or hobbled.'

'Carlos will take care of that. He, too, knows about horses,' Sebastian offered.

Carlos nodded confidently, and Jed smiled.

'Good,' he said, and looked at Billy Newton. 'Now, let's all get clear about what we're doing.'

Within minutes, Jed led them to a twist in the drybed creek. It was less than a quarter-mile from Scranton's camp. Keeping low, they made their way in silence to within fifty yards of the unsuspecting, still-sleeping men.

Jed held up, and signalled for all to dismount. The men climbed quietly from their horses, securing them to the gnarled shrub roots that snagged the shallow banks of the creek. Jed drew his Walker Colt, and instinctively checked for a full chamber. He eased back the hammer, took a final look behind him and moved towards Scranton's posse.

15

Guns at the Creek

Dawn was breaking as Jed tracked quietly through the brush. He was looking for a night guard, taking no chance on there not being one. From ahead of him, a chuckbird peeped, then scuttled, bankside, to the creek. He'd found the guard.

The man was stamping his feet, and gaping into the chill air. Jed recognized him at once. It was Grit Bowler, the river rat from Waco, the man who'd snatched the shotgun from Lena on the stoop at Indian Stone.

It was only then that Jed was sure of it being the Scranton camp, and he felt the scoot of goose bumps along his gun arm. He watched the man closely, assessing the character and situation. He remembered what Billy had said:

'not the sort of man you'd want to take home with you'.

From way back along the creek, Jed heard the soft chortle of one of their horses. Bowler heard it too, and raised his hat against the skyline. Jed wondered if the man could see anything from the higher ground and turned around, but all he could see was the dry creek bed. When he turned back, Bowler had gone, vanished into the brush between the horses and campsite.

Jed swore, and rammed the heel of his hand and gun butt into the side of the creek bed. He'd depended on surprise to help square the odds, but suddenly they'd moved on. He swore again, and with his mind made up for him, he fired once in the air, and broke out after Bowler.

★   ★   ★

By the time Bowler reached campside, men were already crawling from their blankets. Harrel Beggs was first out, turning the cylinder of his pistol. Dawson Cutter rolled on to his knees, and pulled himself up by the loose rein of his horse. He was a long-time badlands campaigner, and never hobbled or tethered his mount into line.

Bowler shouted into Lepe Scranton's ear. The man's response was slow, but sure. He got to his feet and looking around him, stretched. 'Did you see 'em?' he asked Bowler.

'I've seen the horses. They're real close, along the creek bed.'

'What the hell's happenin'?' croaked out Chark Measurer.

'Don't know yet,' Bowler yelled back. 'But they're close enough to know we're here.'

Cutter was pulling on the belly girdle of his saddle. He looked across at Scranton. 'Rangers,' he suggested.

All Scranton's posse had their reasons, and the thought of Texas Rangers flung them into confusion and near panic. With night-stiffened arms and legs they kicked from their night rolls, grabbing for boots and guns.

Scranton rammed his hat on his head and shouted, 'Where the hell they comin' from, Grit?'

Bowler was going to point, but instead he made a grab for his gun. He was staring at the figure of Jed Crane, behind and beyond Scranton. He fired, yelling at the same time, and Scranton threw himself sideways as the blast from two guns roared in his ears.

But Bowler had been hit, and Jed was ready to fire again. Bowler caught another bullet, and the pain spilled from his eyes. He was attempting to twist down, to squeeze the agony from low in his belly. His legs lost control and as he died, he pitched forward helplessly into the smoking embers of the camp-fire.

The camp erupted with unnerved men shouting and cursing. At the same time, a withering hail of rifle fire swept the camp. Jed crouched low for a few seconds, holding both hands tight against his ears. By the noise, Scranton's posse were emptying their guns.

Scranton himself fired three or four times towards Jed. Jed crooked his left arm over his head and raised his eyes. He saw a man lurch between himself and Scranton, only to be crushed by bullets; Billy Newton on one side, Chark Measurer on the other. He watched spellbound, as the man cried out, hit the ground still running.

Scranton fired again, but the hammer of his pistol clinked against the spent cylinder. He threw a glance in Jed's direction and mouthed a few words. Then he turned his back on the uproar.

Jed levelled his Colt at a small belt buckle, low in the middle of Scranton's back. He thought of his brother Milo, his father and the Pinto boys, and bit his lip as Lepe Scranton decided to make a run for it.

Harrel Beggs, Scranton's top hand, had already made it away, along with one or two others. They were the ones who knew too much of dawn ambush to stand and make a fight of it.

Chark Measurer was made of more dogged stuff. With a big Army revolver in his hand, he was staggering backwards, then forwards, as bullets smacked into his body. He tried to yell, but blood surged from his mouth and choked the cry. He raised his gun, firing into the ground ahead of him, then threw it down in disgust. He opened his mouth again, and the sound was thin and reedy, cut off by the impact as more Pinto bullets finally hacked him down.

Jed took a long, deep breath, and stepped out on to clearer ground when Dawson Cutter became a silhouette. He pulled back the hammer of his Colt, and in cold anger pulled the trigger. As Cutter's horse went down, he knew he hadn't made a clean hit. He swore as the man rolled from the saddle and scrambled to his feet to avoid the thrashing forelegs of his stricken mount.

Cutter pulled his gun and looked

wildly around. But Jed had fired again. The second bullet bent Cutter double, then he twisted and fell, dead within clawing distance of his horse.

There was no more shooting then, only the aftermath of pressing silence. Veils of acrid powder smoke curled slowly across the still damp ground, and all Jed could hear was the blunt rumble of running horses. He knew it was Eben Tubbs and Tom Needle running off Scranton's remuda.

He held his Walker Colt down at his side, and looked back into the brush, at the nearest touch of the creek. 'That's it,' he shouted. 'We've done enough. It's over. Move back to the horses.'

He waited awhile, moving among the bodies of the four men; poking at their guns with the toe of his boot. Then he hunkered down and reloaded his Colt. He took a last, cynical look, before making his way back along the edge of the creek.

Sebastian Pinto was talking to Olmedo, and Jed made a significant nod in their direction. He didn't think words were needed. The men mounted their horses, separating out across the range.

Jed rode fast along the line of the creek, not stopping until he was at least a mile from Scranton's shattered camp. He was out of range of any remaining guns, but he waited tensely for Eben Tubbs to get there with the horses. Within minutes, he saw Carlos Pinto and Tom Needle leading them in.

From beside Jed, Billy was asking questions. 'You'll be turning 'em all loose? They won't be all our brands. It'll come close to thievin' if you take 'em.'

'We'll keep all those that belong to us,' Jed replied. 'The others can have a run on the plateau.' He looked at Tubbs and Pinto. 'Take 'em way off. We don't want 'em falling back into the hands of Scranton's pack. In the meantime we've got ourselves some rested mounts.'

Jed and his men were as bushed as

their own horses. Beat and ragged from twelve hours of night-riding and the fight. Yet, they were eager and ready to go on.

With Tom Needle and Carlos, Eben brought up the horses, the bloodied neck scarf showing through his ripped chaps. He grinned through the rind of dirt and stubble on his face. 'Got them all,' he said. 'Some unbroken Pintos, and I got me a mustang back. There's a bunch of Indian Stone. Near thirty in all.'

Billy laughed. 'The bootmaker's gonna make a tidy profit from all those feet trudging into town.'

'Yeah, an' they ain't gonna forget it,' Jed said a tad sharper than he meant. 'Change your saddles, boys. You know what's next, an' we've a journey ahead.'

There was a forty or fifty mile ride ahead of them, and through the best part of the night. McCluskey would have been warned of their approach, and Jed considered the harsh reality of another fight when they caught up. He knew they'd all be near breakdown with tiredness, and the horses would be suffering after the long ride.

Jed tugged firmly on the belly girdle of his fresh mount. If they failed to take the herd, there'd be no outrunning the pursuers; and west of the plateau, the only place to hide would be gopher holes.

16

Moving Out

It was approaching first light and, for a short while, Billy Newton stood off from the herd. He was listening to the night sounds, before cutting a route through the bed-grounded longhorns. Careful not to spook the cattle, he rode through the herd, closer to one of George McCluskey's night riders.

In the dark isolation, he edged his horse in close to the cowboy. He called softly above the contented lowing, 'Hey, mister, what's your name?'

The man was jumpy, fearful, and without thinking, answered simply, 'Stryder.'

Billy smiled sharply. 'You should have stayed abed, Stryder. This ain't the best night to be abroad. Listen to me well.'

The man, Stryder, seemed to accept

the problem he was facing, and sat his horse quietly, as Billy explained what was expected of him.

'The border's south-east of here. I'd say about forty miles. Ride for it now. There'll be no welcome back at your camp, only someone to shoot you.'

Billy whistled gently through his teeth, as the rider turned his horse smartly towards the Texas border. He sat for another minute or two, before cantering around the flank of the herd.

When he made out what he was looking for, he veered away from the cattle for fifty yards; then, with his hand on his gun, he slammed his mount's flanks hard into another of McCluskey's riders.

The man's senses had been numbed by tiredness when the dramatic attack on his pony came. He was jerked into a frightened response. 'What the . . . what's goin' . . . who the hell . . . ?'

Billy gripped the butt of his gun. 'You're goin' home. I've just sent Stryder packin'. You know him?'

The man thought for a second, then made a vain grab for his gun. He fumbled while trying to control his frightened pony.

Billy drew his own gun, casually leaned over, and lashed out at the cowboy's face. There was a dull moan and, as the man fell sideways, his boot-heel caught in the stirrup. The pony snorted, and leaped forward in a blind panic.

Billy grimaced as the cowboy was dragged face down in the soil. Brutal, but better than being dead, Billy thought.

Chew Heddon, the third night rider, had already made the quarter-hour ride back to his camp. He wearily swung a leg from his saddle and his boot had just touched ground when the long barrel of a .44 Walker Colt, stabbed him rudely in the small of his back. The man stiffened, as he felt his gun being lifted from his holster. 'Nice an' easy, cowboy,' Jed said.

'Who the hell are you?' the man responded.

'The man who's takin' his herd back.' Jed moved the man away from his horse, prodding him towards the chuckwagon. 'Don't make a fuss, an' you'll live. Come an' meet some of your friends.'

The camp-fire threw up remaining flickers, and beyond it there was a group of cowhands with tied hands and feet. The Pinto brothers stood guard with rifles.

The man offered his hands to Tom Needle, and then sat down for his boots to be tethered. His colleagues stayed close-mouthed and morose.

Billy Newton rode in, and Jed walked over quickly. He held the snaffle of Billy's horse. 'How's the herd? They quiet?' he asked eagerly.

'Yeah, they're quiet. I saw the night crew off without any trouble. They'll be way gone by now. Them longhorns can still be spooked though, most of 'em are half wild.'

Jed was still worried. 'We'll take a chance they can look after 'emselves for another hour or so.'

He turned to Hash Claymore, the cook, the only McCluskey man who wasn't hog-tied. 'Your job's to get some breakfast goin'.'

'Wasn't expectin' guests at this hour,' he grumbled. 'Fire's down anyways.'

'Then get it started, or I'll do it myself and sit you on it,' Jed snapped.

He narrowed his eyes as Claymore kicked indolently at the dying embers.

Jed tipped a match to the chuck-wagon lamp and, as the light swelled, he rounded on the sitting prisoners. 'Which of you's George McCluskey?'

A tanned, sinewy man with droopy moustaches, met Jed's eyes. 'I'm McCluskey,' he said. 'An' you'll be Crane, no doubt?' he asked with insolent curiosity.

'That's right, and I own most of this herd you're drivin'. If it means anything, I've a letter to prove it.'

'Letters don't mean a mule's ass, to me, cowboy. Word is, you're a killer an' a thief who's on the run. That herd's about as much yours as mine.'

'You've a way with words, McCluskey, but look at it from my point o' view. While you're thinkin' up an excuse for Buck Rule, I'll be busy drivin' the herd. It's beef for the Kansas market, and I'll be takin' payment in Chimney Point.'

'You'll never see the railhead, Crane,' McCluskey said confidently.

Jed grinned. 'Oh, I forgot to mention it, but right now, Beggs and Measurer'll be crossin' the Styx. Scranton's forty miles back. He'll be crossin' the plateau — on foot.'

McCluskey's jaw dropped and the complacent sneer left his face. His men looked at him suspiciously as the meaning sank in.

'That's right, fellas,' Jed responded. 'Your assets have run dry. The only thing that'll beat us to Chimney Point, is next sun-up.'

As he spoke, the cook, Claymore, was emptying the chuckbox of foodstuffs. He looked down at McCluskey, but Jed caught the slyness.

He turned to Billy Newton. 'Billy, have a rummage in the wagon. You'll probably find a shotgun in the flour barrel. Take out everything.'

McCluskey responded, 'What you gonna leave us with?'

Jed looked at him wearily. 'I'll leave you with your lives. It's more than Rule or Scranton ever would.'

While Jed swallowed beans, he considered their next move. Not having slept for forty-eight hours, they were all exhausted, and they'd ridden a fair piece. The horses were run in too, but that mattered less; they could change mounts with the herd remuda.

'Carlos,' he said, 'when you're finished, you and your brother get those cowboys into the chuckwagon. Take 'em east into the plateau. Unload 'em, but bring the horses back.'

Billy helped the boys, and Eben Tubbs pushed two saddles under the seat of the wagon.

Sebastian Pinto walked towards his

son, Carlos. 'Tell them,' he said, sternly.

Carlos levered a shell into the breech of his rifle and looked arrogantly at the tied-in cowboys. 'If anyone moves, they get out and walk. It will be a long way to safety, roped-up with a bullet in your back.'

Sebastian looked at Jed, who returned the amused expression. Jed shouted, 'Catch us up,' then they watched silently as Carlos and Olmedo rode off in the wagon.

Jed wondered whether it was a job he should be doing himself, but he had to organize their moving-out to Chimney Point. He wanted to get there fast, but didn't want to race the herd. Every head would lose weight, and that meant money.

Jed hitched his big Walker Colt. He needed the greenbacks. Then he'd have *two* ways of unsaddling Buckminster Rule.

17

Lawmen at Chimney Point

'That's some stink,' Billy Newton said. They were atop a low rise, two miles out of Chimney Point. He inhaled deeply. 'Hell, Jed, but it's still somethin' to savour.'

The town lay before them, a ripe cow-cauldron of animal pens and rough-timbered buildings. The rail station settled the end of the line that ran 150 miles east through Oklahoma before branching north. On either side of the track, ten of the fifty pens held cattle for the slaughter houses of Kansas City.

For five days, they'd moved the herd at a fair pace without incident. They'd eaten, but not very well. Bandannas were pinched tight around their noses, dust shrouded them, and sweat caked the creases of their skin. Crude and rough as it looked, the men were glad to see the town. All except Jed, who was mindful of his return.

Stiffly, Sebastian Pinto rode up beside him. 'Perhaps now we can go home,' he grated.

Jed gave him a friendly look. 'Perhaps we can, if I get paid. I'll ride in alone. Don't want to raise any curiosity. If it works out, we'll get clear before sundown.'

Billy rode between them. 'Yeah, that means you stayin' away from the Silver Ribbon.'

Jed twitched his reins, and grinned wryly. 'I'm done with lone drinkin', Billy. See yah.' He set his Stetson, and gently spurred his horse.

* * *

Jed found a buyer at the bar of Moses Hotel. A small, dapper man in a suit introduced himself as W.W. Wilkes, of the Kansas Rib Company. Without query, Wilkes accepted Jed's attestation as legal owner, and agreed to value and buy the whole herd. He went immediately to arrange space in the pens, and Jed returned to his campsite.

Later in the afternoon, the cattle were marked down, and penned near the railhead, ready for loading into the cars. Wilkes organized a banker's draft for $10,000, and recommended a buyer for the horses. The few without familiar brands, Eben had turned loose along the Edwards Plateau; the remainder tallied twenty-five head, and Eben sold them to the town's Yankee horsetrader.

Jed deposited the banker's draft at the Oklahoma Cattleman's Bank. He paid in to the credit of Gideon Crane, and drew $2,000 in cash. Out of that, he'd pay Sebastian, Eben Tubbs and Tom Needle.

'Stay away from the west side of town, Mr Crane. They'll kill for a whiskey cork,' the clerk advised.

'I'll be safe enough,' Jed said, 'but thanks.'

It was sound advice. The cow town was popularly known as 'No Point', and had earned it. He stuffed his left hand deep into a buckskin pocket and stepped on to the sidewalk. Thugs and gunmen were one thing, Buck Rule and the law was another. If word was out he was wanted in Texas, it could rouse the interest of a bounty hunter. The boys had gone to Moses Hotel to wait for him. They could take a shave or a bath, maybe both, have a proper meal, and a drink. But they weren't going to stay around long after nightfall.

He walked along to the hotel where he'd left his horse tied-in alongside the others. From the look of the mounts it was obvious they'd recently done some hard travelling. It provoked the interest of two men who were looking at Jed's chestnut gelding.

As he stepped up to the hitching rail, Jed felt the prickly surge of sweat. The men turned casually towards him, their faces expressionless. They both wore long, cotton dusters and dark, sweat-stained hats. One said in a toneless voice, 'Evenin'. This your horse, mister?'

Jed's gut tightened, as he sensed the unmistakable, heavy presence of state lawmen. It was what he'd feared.

He swallowed hard, and rode it out. 'It is,' he said firmly. 'If it's any of your business.'

The man raised his eyebrows fractionally and looked towards his colleague. 'You recall him bein' one of 'em?'

The second man levelled his gaze at Jed. 'It was back in early summer,' he said. 'Don't recall him bein' with 'em then.'

Jed's nerves were clashing. He turned on both men. 'You got somethin' to say, Mister, say it, or let me be.'

'Don't bite just yet, friend,' said the first man. 'I'm Felix Chelloe, County Sheriff. We've some questions need answerin'.'

Again, Jed looked at both men. 'What questions?'

'I see you're Indian Stone. That's Texas. I'd like to know your name?'

'I'm Jed Crane. Indian Stone's my father's ranch. I'm carryin' his note.'

Chelloe sniffed at Jed's response; didn't seem too interested one way or another, but he held out his hand for the paper. Jed felt alongside the wad of dollars for the handwritten document his father had given him. Chelloe stiffened slightly as Jed's hand moved, but the other lawman never flinched as his eyes remained on Jed.

'This ain't the place, Jed,' Chelloe said. 'We'll be more comfortable in my office. Let's go.'

Chelloe handed the paper to his colleague, and indicated for Jed to move along the street. The lawman escorted Jed to his office which was sandwiched between the mail rider's depot and livery stable. It was now early evening, and an oil lamp was already throwing its yellowish glow across a broad, cluttered desk.

The sheriff took back the paper from

his colleague and had a closer look. 'Seems genuine enough,' he said, and returned it to Jed. 'This here's Linus Brooke,' he continued. 'Deputy Marshal, out of Boise City. He's got an interest in your Indian Stone ranch.'

Brooke's cold, dark eyes met Jed's. 'Indian Stone drove a herd up here earlier in the year,' he said flatly.

'Is that a question, or what?' Jed stared back at the deputy marshal. He only saw the man's inflexible intent.

Brooke gave a small, twisted smile. 'It's not the herd I'm interested in, Crane, it's three of the men who came with it. One of them was ridin' that chestnut gelding you say's yours.'

Jed, made the twisted smile in return. 'Yeah, that would have been Buckminster Rule, he's the Sheriff of Juno Flats; big man, bald head, wears black. I'm guessin' that Lepe Scranton, and a young Comanche 'breed were the other two.'

Brooke paused. 'Sounds like 'em,' he said. 'They still riding for you?'

'They never rode for me, they rode for themselves,' Jed cracked back. 'Gato March, the 'breed is dead, and Scranton's walkin' the desert. For all I know, Rule's still plunderin' Langtry County. What's your interest in 'em, Marshal?'

'Murder's top o' the list. They shot a farmer and his family, took their livestock.'

'How d'you know it was them?' Jed wanted to know.

'Took a while for the farmer's wife to die. She talked some. Enough to make it certain. I'd already seen 'em here in town a few weeks before. They're the sort you don't forget.'

'And Rule was one of 'em?' Jed asked doubtfully.

Brooke shrugged. 'As good as. We're certain of the other two.'

Jed's mind started to race. He was on the run from a lawman who was implicated in murder, and wanted by the Federal authority.

Brooke stopped his thoughts. 'You

say these men were never workin' for you?' he queried.

'No, Marshal; not for me. Maybe it looked like Indian Stone, but that's a story. I've been away a long time. I never knew what was going on at Indian Stone, but found it in a real sorry state. My father ain't coping any more. That's where Buck Rule comes in. He thinks bein' Sheriff entitles him to take all that ain't tied down. That includes my father's ranch.'

Chelloe was shuffling some papers on his desk. 'Let me guess,' he said. 'That 'breed you say's dead, and Scranton. You caught up with 'em?'

Chelloe exchanged an amused glance with Brooke. For the first time, Jed sensed some understanding. 'With your permission, Sheriff, I need to get back to Juno Flats and the ranch,' he said.

Chelloe nodded. 'Texas is way beyond my jurisdiction, Crane, but there's a telegraph, and Brooke's Federal. I'm satisfied, an' I've heard enough. But just remember, you'll be having a new state governor down there next year. Time's nearly up for Rule and that free-loadin' rabble.'

As he walked from the sheriff's office towards Moses Hotel, presentiment afforded Jed the sensation of a bullet in the middle of his back. He understood Chelloe's warning about Rule, and next year was too far off.

18

Death of a Marshal

Slumped, big-shouldered in his chair, Buckminster Rule glowered through the window at the sunbaked street. It was mid-afternoon, and the heat of the day was sweeping and oppressive. From where he sat, he couldn't see the lone horseman who rode slowly through the cottonwoods at the edge of town.

Harrel Beggs and Lipper Weems were timekilling. They sat at a small table playing penny-ante with Lepe Scranton. Chum Weems lay on a cot, his hat pulled over his begrimed face. Lipper made a nasal snigger, as he inched a pile of small coins towards him. Scranton twitched irritably.

Without taking his eyes off the deserted street, Rule grumbled, 'Crane knew where you were. How'd he know that?'

'For God's sake, Buck, I didn't hang around to ask 'em. How many more times I gotta tell it? Beggs saw their horses, then they just came outa the creek bed, guns blazin'.'

Scranton was still ornery from his crippling trek back from the plateau. His eyes carded their hurting look, and Rule's constant badgering wearied and bored him. Beggs kept silent, but he, too, was chafing to get even.

Making a column of his coin, Lipper smirked, 'You ain't even got enough for a sodie-pop now, Lepe.'

As the squawk of his voice hung in the air, Scranton gave a look that chilled the dribble on Lipper's chin.

From being sent into the Edwards Plateau without mounts, Scranton, Beggs and three others, had walked near thirty miles, before they'd come across a prospector. The old man had two mules that he'd led down from the Sangre de Cristos. One of the cowboys handed over five dollars, and Scranton and Beggs took a mule each.

Rule had heard nothing from McCluskey; had no idea of what had happened to the herd. He was still wondering if they'd made it to Chimney Point when he noticed the man riding towards his office.

'Looks like we've got a visitor,' he said, and Chum Weems pushed his hat away from his face.

The rider had dismounted and tethered his big bay horse to the hitch rail. Rule twisted in his chair, buckled on his gunbelt, as the man paused to shake out his duster. Against the dipping sun, the man's shadow fell through the open doorway as he stopped to pin up a silver badge. When he looked into the office, Rule saw the set of confidence and hard purpose.

'Well, it's been a while since a US marshal paid us a visit,' Rule said without getting up. 'Must be something of real import.'

The man looked around the sheriff's

office. He looked hard at Scranton, then concentrated on Rule.

'If you're the sheriff, I'm Linus Brooke, Deputy US Marshal. I carry warrants for three men. Two I can use.'

Rule moved around in his chair; instinct made him careful. 'You have names or descriptions, Marshal?'

'Oh sure.' Brooke swept up a shotgun from beneath his long duster. The action was smooth and fast. 'Big man, bald head, wears black. That tells me it's you, Sheriff,' Brooke nodded in the direction of Scranton. 'An' this mean lookin' one with the long hair'll be Lepe Scranton.'

'You reckon you're gonna get to serve them warrants, Marshal?' Scranton hissed.

'I'm here to try, mister.' With his thumb, Brooke eased back the twin hammers. Flicking his gaze from Rule to Scranton, he spoke to Chum Weems. 'You on the cot, just go back to sleep. That way you'll get to wake up.'

Weems puffed, and settled his hat

back into the crust of his beard. Scranton said to the Marshal, 'What are those warrants for?'

'Murder. The Hamm family. Smallholders, on the border. Big mistake leaving the lady alive. She had a good eye for animals.'

Rule pushed himself away from his desk, hands held in front of him. 'Hell, Marshal, none of us been near the border.'

Lipper made to get out from the table. The marshal snapped at him, 'Keep still, kid,' and said to Rule, 'You was there. You and him with the hair, Scranton. Gato March was the Comanche 'breed. There's others in Chimney Point to testify to that.'

Time was running out, and all those in the room knew it. Chum Weems hadn't moved, the only sound was the heavy rattle of his breathing.

Lipper was smiling in callow foolishness, but he knew his father was up to something. With his fingertip, he pushed at the column of coin until it collapsed across the table. A few pennies chinked to the floor, and the tension broke. For the very shortest time, Linus Brooke's attention wavered.

The concussion from the shotgun thundered around the walls of the room and slammed against the ceiling. Linus Brooke sucked in his breath and held it, his face becoming a garish, swollen mask. His head bent forward as if trying to see the enormous blade of the Bowie knife that protruded from low in his throat.

The marshal choked and gargled as he staggered forward, but Beggs had leaped from the table, and was on him. He yanked at the shotgun and, as Brooke fell, he pushed him sideways away from the door. He watched as bright blood crept across the marshal's duster, then turned to Scranton. 'Well done, Lepe, you just killed yourself a US marshal.'

Buck Rule sat immobile in his chair, sweat glistening across his broad face. He rubbed at his nose, sniffing breathlessly. 'Christ, Lepe, how the hell do we get outa this?'

'You're the sheriff, Buck, an' sometimes I wonder if you should be.'

Lipper Weems had a wild attack of sniggering, and Chum Weems rolled off the cot and stood up. He wiped a paw across his hairy face. 'Hell of a place to try an' get some sleep. You've all jus' woke up half o' Boot Hill.'

Astonished, Lipper jigged over to the marshal. As he bent to retrieve Beggs's knife, Chum shouted, 'Leave it, Lipper, there's enough of a mess already.'

Rule was staring out into the street, waiting for the first signs of interest. He was thinking as fast as he could, trying to gain some composure. 'Shouldn't be any problem for a while,' he said.

Harrel Beggs's eyes narrowed, and he looked at Rule doubtfully. 'For a while?' he echoed. 'I reckon your time as sheriff's just run out, Buck.'

Scranton joined in with his own thoughts. 'Yeah, Buck. I'm tiring o' this whole business. We ain't got anything yet. When Brooke don't turn up, there'll be a whole bunch o' US marshals down here; and Crane's still out there somewhere. There's big trouble for us all, *right now*.'

Rule grunted, staring uncertainly at the body of Brooke. 'Pull him into the back room, Lipper. After dark, take him out a few miles.'

Chum Weems was looking out at the marshal's bay mount. 'You gonna ride his horse, Buck? It's sure big enough.'

Lipper poked his head out the door. 'I'll take 'em both, but what we gonna do then?'

Scranton looked from Beggs to Rule. 'I say we ride to Indian Stone. You've unfinished business there, Buck.'

Rule watched as Lipper dragged Brooke across the rough planked floor. 'That's right. I'll get something outa this mess.'

'You'll be thinkin' o' that girl, Buck?' Chum Weems cackled.

'Yeah, and the Crane boy. He'll turn up sooner or later. You're right, Lepe;

we've made nothin' so far, might as well get some satisfaction.'

'That'll be for you, Buck. Just don't forget the rat pocket you tore open, mouthin' off about that girl's bloodline. There's folk around here once looked up to the Crane family. If there's any shame, they'll wanna make it 'emselves.'

'Let 'em then.' Rule slammed his Stetson back on his gleaming bald head. 'Seems it's all a bit late to go worryin' about what the folk round here think.'

19

Journey Home

Four days after leaving Chimney Point, Jed Crane's outfit was back across the North Canadian. Through the hard, grinding land, they continued south, discreet and vigilant. They were outlawed in Texas, and strangers brought the risk of trouble, but they saw no one, and no one saw them.

Jed rode up front. With Indian skill, he used vagaries of light, and the natural shape of the land to provide cover. For ten more days they travelled, making use of hollows and dried-out arroyos. It was when they were camped along an upper reach of the Pecos, with its rising water, that Jed had the premonition, a gut sensation of impending grief for Indian Stone.

★　★　★

It took them five more days to reach the low bluff that overlooked the ranch. Jed reined in and scanned ahead. It was approaching midday, and the sun was climbing into its charring zone. From where he sat, the ranch house was too distant to be made out clearly, its adobe whiteness wavering in the haze off the land. But from across the peaks of the Glass Mountains, grey clouds had formed, and Jed watched the leaden sky, as it rolled eastwards. Waiting patiently while the others rode into file alongside him, he wondered how long, before a storm slammed into the range.

'I'll go in alone from the east, Billy,' he said. 'You and the others come in from the west.' The mood was telling, but nobody queried their purpose.

Tense and strung-up, Jed heeled the gelding into a canter. After a few minutes he stopped to watch a plume of dark smoke coil its way up to a lone, turkey buzzard. The icy grip of fear returned to the pit of his stomach.

He kicked the horse into a gallop, making for the tangles of mesquite that pitted the land near the house. It was near reckless flight, and Jed paid scant attention to the likelihood of ambush. He leapt from the saddle and ran forward with the horse. There was no sign of life, only the strong, drifting smell of burning. He turned upwind, and from the edge of the yard, he stared, numbed, at the ranch house.

Around the doorway and windows the adobe walls were sooted black. Most of the roof was gone, charred beams angled into the sky. The stone chimney rose from the pile of smouldering tile where the roof had fallen in. He pulled his horse forward, his Walker Colt gripped in his right hand.

He stood beside the corral rails and stared at the beaten-up ground where horses had panicked to get out. The broken corpse of one small cowpony lay in the yard, its limbs stretched taut. For a full minute he listened, but there was no sound other than the crackle of searing wood. He looked at the blackened, smoking ruin that had once been his home.

In the gap between the door posts, his father's laprug was wrapped around the wheel of his toppled chair. His gaze wandered, noting detail with cold anger. The stoop was littered with pots, dishes and household things, all smashed to rubble. They'd looted the place before burning it.

He stood, horrified. What had happened to his father and Rafelena? Where were they? The reins dropped from his fingers and he took a step towards the porch. Family possessions had been piled in the middle of the front room and torched. The kitchen, and back bedrooms weren't badly damaged, and he turned to see that the barn and outbuildings were untouched. He stooped, ran a finger around the rim of a hoof print, and looked hard into the distance.

He heard the sound from off to his

left, near a short run of toolsheds. He rolled forward into the ground turning on his side, his arm outstretched, the Colt steady in his hand.

'Get out here,' he bellowed. 'Get into the open, or I'll come find you.' He raised himself on one knee and gripped the Colt with both hands. His voice dropped, contorted with rage. 'Believe me, you'll die real painful.'

'Don't shoot, Jed. Please, don't shoot.' From a tight gap between two sheds, Lena reeled into the yard. She fell to her knees, ashen, every nerve and sinew dragging her down.

'Lena,' Jed yelled, running towards her. 'Where is everybody? Where's my father?'

Lena clawed her fingers across her smeared, swollen face, and Jed, crouching before her, laid his gun on the ground.

'I'm sorry, are you hurt? he asked, intensely.

She shook her head wretchedly, and fought for the words. 'No, I'm all right

. . . It's your father . . . ' She held up a trembling arm. 'I think he's in there . . . I think they killed him, Jed.'

Lena's voice beat around Jed's head as he ran, oblivious to the lacerating claw of the mesquite. The body lay across the exposed roots of a gnarled cottonwood, and Jed was rasping as he looked down on the fuzzed, gaunt face of his father. The old man's eyes were closed, and his skin was thin and limpid. It was almost the face of a stranger, except for the long nose and hostile clench of his jaw. Jed took a few deep breaths, his heart was thumping. He knelt and placed his fingers gently between where blood had welled then dried in patches across Gideon's broken chest.

That was it. It didn't really matter about anyone else; it would be for his father, that men would die. All those responsible for the hardship and torment they'd wreaked upon the old man.

Faltering, and in tears, Lena poured out what had happened.

'It was still dark, very early . . . there was noise from the corral. I thought it was you and Billy come back. But there were more horses in the yard . . . I got out of bed to see what was happening. Gideon was there, pulling open the front door . . . I could see his shotgun in his lap. There were men making so much noise. Gideon shouted, then fired out at them. I couldn't see anything . . . it was too dark . . . he was in the doorway.'

Jed looked across at the charred framework of the door and his father's blanket. 'What happened then? What happened to you?'

'There was lots of shooting . . . bullets came through the door as well. I hid back in my room. Gideon was hit . . . I heard it . . . the terrible sound. I could still see through my door. Buckminster Rule was there. I heard his voice. Then they drove off the horses. One of them came up the steps . . . he dragged Gideon away. I only found him when they'd gone. I couldn't do anything . . . didn't know what to do.'

'Yeah, I can imagine,' Jed said, distractedly. He was already thinking that he'd have to leave the girl there for a while; she was the best person to tend his father.

From the corner of his eye he caught the sudden, uneasy movement of his horse as four riders galloped in across the yard. Billy Newton was leading, his eyes flashing.

'What the hell, Jed?' He looked unbelievingly at Lena, then at the burned ranch house. 'Where's the old man?'

'They killed him. He's in the brush.'

'Who, Rule?'

Jed was trying to throw off his shock. 'Yeah, him or his men. From the look of it, all of 'em.'

Pulling off his battered sombrero, Sebastian Pinto rode his criollo up close. His dark eyes burned fiercely, but he was in control, and his manner was one of patient understanding.

'Olmedo will take the lady to Cactus Rose,' he said to Jed. 'He can send back *vaqueros*. Carlos will stay here and take care of your father's body. I will ride with you now.'

Jed didn't feel like talk any more. He watched as Carlos dismounted to offer up the reins.

'No,' Lena said, 'I'm staying here. It's been my home for a long time now; and there's some livestock left that still needs feeding.' She tried a small smile, and looked up at Sebastian. 'It would be very kind, if you helped me with Gideon, but then I'd like to be alone. Go with Carlos, then bring some help. There's no one coming back here for a while. What would they want?'

Jed looked at the stunned faces around him. 'You all know where I'm going. If you're still with me, Billy, we'll ride now.'

Without turning back, the two men

rode from the yard. They were headed due south, into the looming rain, and Juno Springs.

Half-way to the town, Jed reined up, sharply swinging his horse in a tight circle. He turned to Billy, and shouted, 'This is all wrong, Billy. Get back to the ranch. They're gonna return. Scranton and Beggs; Weems as well, maybe. It's not the ranch they want any more — that's why they didn't worry about setting fire to it — it's personal. Look out for Lena, they'll want her, too. Meet me out beyond the cottonwoods when I return. Get going.'

It was a big rain that moved fast from the foothills of the Glass Mountains, and Jed felt behind his saddle for a slicker.

20

Confrontation with a Lawman

Buckminster Rule yawned and stretched himself in his chair. He swung his legs up and propped them on the edge of the desk. The water trickled down the walls from the warped shakes, and the failed daylight irritated him. He considered going over to Wagnall's for an early snifter. He snatched up his hat and stepped from the office. He looked along to the saloon, then across the street. In less than an hour, the hard-packed mud had become a churned lake. There was just a thin, yellow light set back in Buffer's hardware store, and Buck grinned, oilily. He pulled up his collar, and pulled the door to, behind him. If Buffer had something for a thirst, he'd get his deputy, Turl O'Brien, to look after the town for the rest of the night.

* * *

It was full dark when Jed reined in at the north end of Juno Flats. He dismounted quietly, and hitched his horse to a collapsed rig.

The town seemed to be in hiding from the storm, the main street lying silent and empty before him. A light shone outside Wickett's Saloon, but the place wasn't busy, and most of the town's other buildings were in drenched darkness.

There was a lamp in the livery barn, and he could see a mule snatching at a hay pile. The blacksmith was whittling and, as Jed approached, he gave a slight look of annoyance at being disturbed. Jed was bereft of any nicety, and stepped up quickly beside the man's chair. He grabbed at a heavy, wool vest, and dragged the surprised smithy to his feet.

'I don't aim to disturb you for long. I'm looking for the sheriff. You'd know if he's in town; I want to know where he is.'

The man stared at him truculently, but didn't reply. Jed could see the fear in the man's eyes that flicked to the shotgun resting against an animal cage.

'I just want to know where he is. I can beat it out of you if I have to.'

'He'll kill me, if he finds out I told you.'

Jed methodically pulled the Walker Colt from around his waist, and ran the barrel around the base of the smithy's jaw. 'For Chris'sake, *I'll* kill you *now* if you don't tell me.'

'Try Buffer Wagnall, across from the saloon. That's where he goes most nights.'

Jed's manner was emotionless. He released his hold and stepped back a pace. 'Where's the deputy?'

'He'll be over at the jail.'

Jed cast a quick glance at the shotgun. 'It'd be a real smart move if you carried on with your carving for a while.'

The smithy dropped back into his chair. 'I wasn't thinking of going anywhere.'

It was a half-hour later, when Rule returned to his office. He locked the door behind him, and shed his coat and hat. He was going back to his chair, when Jed Crane confronted him from the store-room.

Rule groaned, as the muzzle of a Colt .44 gaped at his broad, glistening forehead.

Before he spoke, Jed waited while thunder crashed its way across town. Then he said quietly, 'Who was it shot my father, Rule?'

The sheriff's eyes bulged with sudden fear, as Jed pushed the barrel of his Walker Colt against his stomach. 'Tell me who shot my father,' Jed repeated.

Rule's blood drained. 'That's nothing to do with me.'

'Everything that happens here is to do with you, Rule. Tell me who pulled the trigger, you sonofabitch.'

He pushed his left hand up tightly under Rule's throat. He gripped,

203

pushing backwards until the big man stumbled awkwardly into his chair. The sheriff was sweating, and shaking uncontrollably.

Jed thumbed back the hammer of the Colt. 'I'll push the barrel in real deep, Sheriff. That way nobody'll hear the bang when I pull the trigger.'

'It was Scranton,' Rule gasped.

Jed swore under his breath. He stared at the floor between Rule's boots, then looked around the office. There was a shotgun lying across the top of an empty stove, and a bottle with an inch of pine-top on the table. He picked it up and had a mouthful. Then he pushed his Colt back in his waistband and cleaned his hands with the remaining liquid.

He turned his head as if to say something, then back-turned the key in the door lock. He stood for a short while in the doorway, considering. Above the roar of the rain, he heard Rule move, and turned to face him.

The sheriff was standing in the far

corner of his office, the shotgun gripped tightly and pointed at Jed. 'You'll be back for me, Crane, we both know it. I can't let you walk away,' he said, almost tragically.

Jed made no reply; he understood Rule's dilemma. He stepped out into the deluge, with nothing but contempt and disgust for the sheriff. It was only when he heard the distinctive click of the shotgun's twin hammers that he turned, his hand scarcely moving inside his soaking slicker.

Buckminster Rule was a grasping opportunist, not a cold-blooded killer, and didn't fire when he should have. He jerked back as Jed's bullet struck him in the chest. He took the impact with a violent, backwards jerk, then he pitched forward. As his eyes clouded, he didn't even summon up the strength to trigger the shotgun. Jed shuddered at the thought of the man's big, meaty face slamming into the damp floorboards of his own office.

Jed glanced at the body in disbelief,

then at the torn, blackened hole in the front of his slicker. His top lip twisted cynically. 'Whatever it was you wanted, sheriff you must have thought it was worth dying for.'

He walked fast, back to his horse, and didn't look back.

21

Into Hiding

Jed's horse snorted alarm, and he slowed him to a trot. Through the incessant hiss of rain he heard the faint clip of another horse. He listened for a moment trying to locate a figure. He was disorientated, but decided the sound was coming from the direction of Indian Stone ranch. He held his horse in tight and waited, still and silent.

The rider was keeping to the wagon road that trailed back towards Juno Flats. Jed's mare snorted loudly again, and he jerked the reins and made hush noises. But the man on the horse had pulled away from the trail to locate the sound. Through the rain that had brightened with the dawn light, he came close. He saw Hed's blurred shape, and walked slowly towards him.

'Jed. Jed Crane,' he called.

Under his slicker, Jed eased forward the hammer of his Colt, and pushed the gun back into his waistband. 'You're takin' a chance,' he muttered. He recognized the voice of Billy Newton.

'And you came close to bein' dead,' Billy shouted back, hooking his gun back into his holster. He edged his mount closer. 'They've come back, Jed. You were right. I decided to ride out and find you. Couldn't tell where the hell I was goin', using the trail as a marker. I got away without them seein' me, but Lena's still there.'

Jed kneed his horse as it swung around, restless, under the unbroken pelt of rain. He stared into the misty range. 'I'll go and get her then.'

'There's at least four of 'em, Jed. They'll be looking out for 'emselves. Just waiting for you.'

'Trying to scare me, Billy?'

'No. I'm coming in with you. There'll be nothing here for me, if I don't. Your old man never did any harm to no one.

He helped me an' your Sully, when we had our great, sappy ideas.'

Billy nodded with finality, and Jed smiled understandingly. 'Perhaps we've wasted enough time.'

'Yeah,' Billy said. 'Sometime, you can tell me what you did to Buck Rule.' He threw a doubtful glance at Jed. 'My pa once told me there'd be days like this.'

* * *

Rafelena stirred slightly, sighed and opened her eyes. As she twisted and glanced about her, reality crept in, her memory returned. Six hours before, she'd rolled herself into a blanket. Under the unbroken drum of rain, and out of despair, she'd fallen asleep on her bed.

She heard sounds from out front of the house, and swung her legs on to the floor. She recognized the voices of the men who had brought the burning and death to Indian Stone; the voices she'd thought gone.

She drew a leather jerkin and a pair of boots from her wardrobe. At the back of the cupboard she grabbed the .38 Yellowboy. She crossed to the window, raised a corner of the drawn blind, and peered out. There was a tinge of dawn-grey creeping in from the east, and the land was filled with torrential rain. It slanted into the room around her feet as she raised the wooden frame.

She crouched beneath the window-sill, and water sluiced in a cold edge across her neck. She couldn't see beyond the livery stable, and decided to try for an annexed toolshed. She was soaked, alone and frightened. Eventually, one of the Weemses or Lepe Scranton would come looking for her, and the ranch would be tooth-combed.

She levered a shell into the carbine. The ranch was her home, and, for the first time, she felt totally alone and vulnerable.

22

Retaliation

The horses were tethered inside a protective brake of cottonwood. The ground was soft and muddy, and under cover of the rain, there was little fear of being seen from the burnt, sodden remains of the ranch house.

Keeping low, the two men made their way forward. It took them fifteen minutes to reach the edge of the yard. Although daylight had increased, visibility had worsened to less than fifty feet.

Billy looked suddenly worried, and he'd started to shiver. 'Where do you reckon they are, Jed?'

'Don't know. There'll be one of 'em looking out front, an' another out back, but they'll be under cover.'

Billy stared gloomily around him, but

the rain fractured all visibility. They couldn't see any of the ranch house buildings.

Jed stared at him hard. 'You can ride away, Billy. There ain't nothin' wrong with wantin' to see the end of the day.'

'Nah, I'm stayin'. I'll go back a bit, get around the side of the sheds. D'ya think Lena'll be in the house, Jed?'

'Yeah, I guess so. They'll have her cooped up, somewhere.'

The words were cut short, as a great thunderclap crushed the sky above them. Jed trembled instinctively, then looked up to see Billy ducking off and away to his left.

★   ★   ★

Billy Newton steadied his tense muscles. He tunnelled his eyes straight ahead, but relaxed for the slightest movement to show. Like Jed, he wanted retaliation and, as the tautness ebbed, he walked resolutely into the full body of rain. There was movement ahead of him, and he swung his pistol to cover. It was his reflection, fluttering thin and watery from a cracked window. He sidled over to the wall of a storehouse that spurred from the livery stable. He expected some sort of sign, or noise, but nothing moved, and he stepped back into the open. He wondered if Rule's men had decided to pull out while there was still time, but doubted it.

Slowly he moved back to the storehouse. The storm's power was growing, and under its intensity an unbroken spread of noise fell into him from every side. He pondered on Beggs, Lepe Scranton or the Weemses being hidden in the lee of one of the ranch buildings, ready to shoot him without warning.

He turned his back to the open door, and didn't hear the movement behind him. He just caught a timber creak, then the clack of a shotgun hammer as it fell against an inactive cartridge. His body contracted, half waiting for the searing red punch, but it didn't happen.

He whirled to face Lipper Weems. The young nit-brain was staring with disbelief at his gun's misfire.

Billy hurled himself at Lipper. They went down in a heap with legs and arms kicking wildly. Billy felt a sharp pain, deep in his side, but held on to his pistol as he staggered to his feet. Lipper had thrown the shotgun, in favour of a bloodied skinning-knife. He crouched, gathering himself, but he knew he was beaten and, as he leapt, Billy stretched out his arm and fired.

With a bullet through his skull, Lipper buffered into Billy as he came forward. With one hand, Billy gripped at the pain in his side as, still clutching the knife, Lipper's arm whirled into him. He staggered into the doorway, feeling the cold agony of the blade slicing deep along his gun arm. The boy who was about to become a killer, lay spreadeagled at his feet. Billy was breathing in spasms. Then his gun dropped from his fingers and he crumpled into unconsciousness.

With his face pressed into the ground, Billy didn't understand the point of pressure, low against his spine. It was when he twisted his head that he grunted in despair. It was all the time he had, before pain exploded and blackness took him again.

Harrel Beggs laid his rifle on the ground, and tied Billy's hands with a strip of rawhide. He made a noise of satisfaction as he jerked the knot tighter, then he straightened up and stood back. He'd pulled the front of Billy's vest up high, and jammed it into his mouth to prevent him calling out when his senses returned. Finally, Beggs dragged Billy to his feet, and sat him, propped against a barrel in the open doorway of the storehouse.

★ ★ ★

The reverberation of Billy's gun had flattened Jed into the yard that was already inches deep in water.

The gunshot had to be trouble for Billy, and Jed made his move. He raised himself quickly, and ran diagonally for the frameworks of a cluster of stores and sheds. They were no more than a grey, featureless barrier, but ahead of him, Jed picked out the darkness of shadow above an open doorway. He couldn't make a clear picture, only that he seemed to have the advantage of surprise as he bore down on a figure, crouching low.

From behind the cover of Billy, Harrel Beggs fired. The bullet brushed Jed's neck, forcing him sideways, then down on to one knee. By then his Colt had found the indistinct shape of the bloody figure in the doorway, and he pulled the trigger.

Through a pulse of solid rain, Jed saw Billy's face snap up as the bullet hit him, as for a split-second, consciousness and feeling returned to his ally.

Jed's eyes blazed with the instant terror of what had happened. He yelled uselessly, as Billy was hammered back into the doorway. He pounded the Colt into his leg with anger and frustration. There was nothing he could do; Billy's body was already lifeless. He forced himself to take long, deep breaths as he backed off. He now had to concentrate on taking out Scranton's men alone.

Beggs had already left the storehouse through a back door. He looked around him, then slithered along the grey shadows of the outbuildings, back to the company of Chum Weems and Lepe Scranton.

Jed wondered how long it would be before the gunfire brought them out for him. He backed off, looking for a gap between shimmering, adobe walls.

★   ★   ★

Under the charred, partly exposed, roof of the ranch house, Chum Weems and Lepe Scranton were standing close to the windows that fronted the yard. After the shooting, they were waiting for Harrel Beggs to return.

Weems looked across at Scranton. 'How many shots you heard?'

Scranton turned the cylinder of his Colt, smiling at the small, clear clicks it made. 'The same as you. Three,' he said.

'You sure?'

'Yeah, I'm sure.'

'What the hell's happenin' out there? You reckon it's Crane? You reckon he brought help? Those Pintos? Beggs should have finished him off. You heard my Lipper's shotgun?'

Scranton slipped the Colt in its holster, put the gunbelt around his waist and felt the gun's solid weight against his hip. 'No. Don't know who's shootin' who. You'll have to go out there and find out.' He griinned, then laughed. 'I wonder if Crane's met up with Buck? That man ain't come back here to marry either one of us.'

They both knew that Weems was choking back a fear of being 'pigged' in the crossfire between Beggs and Jed Crane.

Scranton was tired of the wait. He grabbed Weems's Stetson and slicker and threw them to him. 'Fer Chris'sake, Chum, let's go get him.' He saw himself in a cracked, hanging mirror, and adjusted his gunbelt. 'I don't reckon on being out there long enough to get wet,' he scoffed.

Ahead of Weems, Scranton grabbed a Winchester, and stepped out on to the stoop of the ranch house. He was instantly soaked to the skin, but didn't appear to notice. There was an incessant run of water around his face, and the ground in front of him had become a foaming sea of water. He was waiting for Weems to join him, and shouted, 'What the hell you doin' in there, Chum? You afraid of gettin' wet, or is it somethin' else?'

Weems appeared in the doorway. 'I wanna know where the girl is. She's got that carbine, remember?'

The two men stood, stared around,

but they couldn't see the livery stable or the adjoining buildings. There was a short, sharp hiss, and Beggs edged towards them, close in to the front of the charred porch. He nodded in the direction of the worksheds.

23

The Shoot-Out

The thunder rolled east, but in twelve hours the solid deluge of rain had flooded the enclosure of Indian Stone to ten swollen acres of waterflats. Barrel staves, fence rails and drowned rats, drifted and bobbed. There was no sound other than the hiss of falling water.

Rain funnelled down from the roofs of the outbuildings where Jed was waiting patiently. He knew his only chance was to take all three men on his own terms. He wasn't going to be rushed; he would take advantage of the weather and the territory.

From the cover of a fodder pen, he was watching as water flashed and spouted from the drooping brim of Chum Weems's Stetson. Dragging the battered brim down low, Weems was waving for Scranton and Beggs to spread. He was carrying a Springfield carbine and a Colt.

Jed edged himself forward, hardly one pace, through a sliding sheet of water. It streamed from his head and filled his ears, and the crash of rain turned blunt and muffled. He flicked his head sharply from side to side and hefted his Walker Colt, wrapping its cinch tight around his wrist. He didn't intend to 'call' these men; no telegraphed invitations. It was one against three, and he had to start the shooting. He brought up the gun and stood sideways on, his body partially hidden by a broken, swinging door.

He watched Beggs, as he backed away from Weems and Scranton, as he stepped into the broken spokes of a rig wheel. Beggs cursed and, as he jerked at his foot, he briefly lost his balance. It was a difficult shot, but the chance that Jed needed.

He fired low into the body of Beggs,

knowing that at least he'd go down. The man dropped his rifle, clutched his groin and span towards Jed, trying to penetrate the rain. His foot was still wedged, and he fell flat, stretched across the half-submerged wheel.

A barrage of lead from Weems's carbine immediately crashed into the pen, splintering loose planks and fragmenting feed sacks.

Jed slithered sideways along the adobe walls, then made a headlong dash for another shed. As he ran across the open ground, he heard Weems shout a warning. He glanced over his shoulder, and saw two figures burst out from either side of the barn, and Weems yelled again.

Weems was running, pointing backwards towards the sheds, when the bullet took him in the back of the neck. He stopped, straightened up, then staggered back with short staccato steps. He buckled sideways, his big hands grappling at Lepe Scranton's gunbelt, then he collapsed, his throat a spiralling wash of pink and red.

Scranton shoved himself free, and brought his rifle to bear on Jed's running figure. Ahead of him, Jed saw a window-frame shatter as he skewed towards the stable. Breath was rasping in his throat, and bullets were tearing into the woodwork ahead of him.

He backed into an open doorway, listening for the frenzied slash of Scranton's feet through water. Jed was unsure of who else was out there; unsure of who'd shot Chum Weems. But he only heard the continuing sound of rain, and from somewhere, the irked yelp of a wretched mongrel. He blew water from the chambers of his Colt. He knew the killer wouldn't follow him into the dread of an outbuilding. Beggs and Weems were already down, and Scranton didn't want to be next.

Under cover of overhangs and stacked timbers, Jed worked his way to within fifty feet of the livery stable. Visibility was just that far, and he could make out the grain-gate in the end of the upper storey. Above the stalls was a risky position with no way out, but he could look down. He heard the Winchester roar from close by, and felt a thump above his elbow, then pain, as the scorch bruised into his upper arm. He sucked in a deep breath and grazed the wound with the barrel of his Colt. The pain wouldn't get any worse than that.

Scranton, now having marked him, was comparatively safe, and more sure of himself. Another bullet clanged, and whined off an iron hitching rail that ran near the stable. Jed made his move. As he ran across the open ground, he turned to see Scranton emerge from between the sheds.

Jed veered into the livery stable. He jumped on to the top of an empty crate and rolled himself awkwardly into the low rafters of the hay loft. The straw was decaying, and the grain bags were swollen and musty. Jed let his Colt hang on its cinch, and he grabbed at the tie-rope of one of the sacks. He levered himself into a sitting position, and shouldered one of the heavy bags into a corner of the grain-gate.

Down below, Gideon's old wagon mule stomped nervously in its stall. Jed fell painfully on to his right shoulder and gathered his Colt into his waist. He looked down, and saw a rat gnawing at a chicken that lay lifeless in a wooden crate. He grimaced, and pointed the long barrel of his Colt down at the rat, cocked the hammer and took deliberate aim.

He turned away as the rat exploded beneath him. Fur scraps and a crimson bloom burst into the mud, and the crash bellowed around the stable.

Jed knew that it was only a matter of seconds before Scranton wondered about the noise. Another hail of bullets was the response, and Jed slid back into the piled up straw. Sweat ran into his eyes, and he rubbed it away with the crook of his arm. He clambered quickly from the loft, wincing from his wound and the withering fire that immediately poured up through the grain-gate. Hanks of roofing were being torn away, and the rain shafted through the stringers. The mule was lashing out at the rear of his stall, and his pale eyes bulged with fright. Manure beneath its feet was steaming fresh, and tufted lumps splattered up and touched Jed's hands and face.

Then nothing moved. The flood water had spread through the stable, and more rats were weaving through the garbage. From the rear door, Jed stood very still, peering intently into the rain that drilled down a few inches from his face.

After a full minute, he made out the blurry figure of Scranton move from the cover of the sheds. He was staring about him nervously, his hands clutched tight around the Winchester. He was trying to make a fix on the gunshot, and Jed's eyes ached, as he watched him.

Jed couldn't bear the suspense, and

he shouted almost in desperation, 'It's the way you'd want it, killer. No chance.'

Scranton stopped in mid-stride as Jed's first bullet hit him in the chest. He snapped forward as the second broke his rifle and half an arm at the same time. There was an expression of astonishment on his face as he stared down at bones that were jelled to the stock and trigger guard. With his other hand he tried to reach for his Colt, then he closed his eyes and fell. He turned over as slow as a timbered log, rain and mud slipping from the rictus of his face. He mouthed something across at Jed, but his pale, empty eyes didn't open again. Only his boots moved, spurs digging the water in frustration and defeat.

Jed swiped his hand at the humidity and thick buzz of saw-flies. He scraped wet filth down from his hair across his face. He blinked some clearness back into his eyes, and pushed the Colt back into his waistband.

He walked into the rain that was still chopping up all sound. In the swirling water, a small garter snake swam into the poncho that bloated around Beggs's neck. From lower down the man's body, a darker ribbon spread slowly, almost touching Jed.

Chum Weems's body was wrapped and shrouded beneath his slicker. His hat was trapped floating, and covered the top part of his face. His eyes would be staring upward, unseeing, and his mouth was open, filling with bright, clean water.

If Billy was alive, Jed would have told him that Weems had got to bathe at last.

In the open doorway of a toolshed, Lena was leaning forward, her face drained like chalk. Cold and shocked, she stared out at the bodies, her lips trembling, trying to force a sound. The .38 Yellowboy carbine dropped from her fingers, and it clattered off the floor of the shed, before splashing under the water. She took a faltering step towards

24

Facing-Up

Since the terrible conflict, Lena and Jed had been living at Cactus Rose. They hadn't spoken much; Lena was troubled by her shooting of Chum Weems, and Jed was tormented by his part in the death of Billy Newton.

Lena took a horse to the range, and for nearly a month they'd made work of rounding-up cattle with Sebastian Pinto and his sons. Eben Tubbs and Tom Needle had helped, before riding north to Colorado. From the cattle that Rule's rustlers had missed, there was enough mavericks and yearlings for Jed to build up a small herd.

Jed was still outlawed in Langtry County, although a marshal from San Angelo, and a telegraph from Felix Chelloe in Chimney Point, had told him there'd likely be no charges brought.

Jed and Lena had just found out that following Gideon's accident, the old man had willed Indian Stone to Lena. Later that same night, they sat on the stoop talking it over.

'The ranch is yours by right, Jed.' Lena was watching fireflies dance along the edge of the arroyo. 'He didn't even know you were alive when he wrote it.'

'Maybe there was a time, Lena, but not any more. There's no place for me here, now.'

There was a short silence, then Lena turned and looked closely at Jed. 'You knew about me, didn't you? Before Rule started the talk?'

Jed nodded and gave a long time-coming smile. 'Yeah, I knew. Dad told me. I don't know why he never told you. If he'd known about me, *that* would have been a reason. Who'd want me for a half-brother?'

'Why do you say that, Jed? Lena asked.

Jed thought for a moment. 'You've heard of the Federal Bounty, Lena?'

'Yes, I think so. Money paid to confederate prisoners who changed sides. They were sent West, to fight Indians, weren't they?'

'Yeah, that's it, sort of. Well, I was one of those who took it.'

Lena looked at Jed with no trace of contempt and he carried on.

'Texans don't take too kindly to any man who did that.' Jed clenched his fists, and turned his face to the night sky. 'But they won't be Texans who were forced to waste away in their own filth . . . starve to death, with their teeth falling from their heads . . . the likes of Scranton stealin' clothes from their backs, so's they could toss 'em naked and scurvy into a pit. They won't be the one's who . . . '

Jed stopped himself. Lena thought it was the pain of remembering.

'I wasn't the only one with a will to live, Lena. But there's few in Langtry County that'll see it that way.' Jed was picking at the floor of the stoop beside him. 'Even with the worst now gone, it'll be a while before this county's right fit to live in.' He looked up at Lena. 'All considered, there's not a lot to stay for.'

'Not a lot to leave either,' Lena said, quiet and meaningful.

'Wonder how much those few cattle'll bring?' Jed mused. Then he said seriously, 'Added to the eight thousand dollars in the Cattleman's Bank, there's enough to start up a business . . . a peaceable, family business.'

'Where?' Lena asked, interested. 'A long ways from here, I wager.'

There was silence for a moment, then Jed flicked a small piece of wood out beyond his boot tips. 'I've been thinkin' of the Yukon,' he suggested, and they smiled together.